For Better or for Worse

A SWEET COASTAL KISSES NOVEL

DANA LeCHEMINANT

Copyright © 2024 by Dana LeCheminant
Cover Design Copyright © 2024 by Karyssa Adair

ISBN: 978-1-951753-25-2
First Print Edition: May 2024
Bow and Arrow Press
All rights reserved.

Chapter One

King

It's not every day you're late to work because a llama got himself stuck in a pool. Except, this isn't the first time this has happened, so that whole 'every day' thing is becoming more and more likely. And while the llama is perfectly fine, if a little waterlogged, I'm at the end of my rope as I storm into the bakery smelling of wet camelid. Not a good smell, if you're curious.

"King!" Meg, the only other morning employee at the bakery, practically screams my name when I stomp into the kitchen. She's too easily startled, especially when she refuses to stop listening to music at full blast whenever she's in the back, and she presses a flour-covered hand to her chest as she heaves in lungfuls of air. "I tried calling you."

I curse under my breath when I realize I left my phone at home, thanks to Prince Harry and his severe lack of self-preservation. I swear, that llama is going to do me in one of these days if he doesn't do himself in first. "Sorry," I mumble and peel off my wet shirt. I could have changed before leaving the house, but

I'm already several weeks behind on laundry as it is, and I'm not sure I would have found a clean shirt.

I had planned to do a load last night after I got home from the surf shop, but I made the mistake of sitting down to eat my microwaved dinner. I woke this morning with a half-eaten meal on my lap and a llama making ungodly noises as he struggled to keep his head above water. Honestly, I have no idea how long he was in the pool before I jumped in to save him.

Despite his impressive ability to escape his pen, Prince Harry is not a smart animal. If he had moved to the other end of the pool, his neck would have been plenty long enough to allow easy breathing. But no, my idiot llama chose the six-foot end, which is just a few inches taller than his nose.

"You okay?" Meg asks, her voice thin.

I glance over at her, wet shirt in hand, and immediately regret my thoughtless decision to remove my shirt. She's doing her best to keep her eyes on mine, but her gaze keeps slipping downward. Meg was honestly a godsend when she applied for the open baker position. She just graduated college and is back home in Willow Cove for the summer until she starts an internship in the fall, and she has enough rudimentary baking skills to follow a basic recipe, plus availability in the mornings. I've got two teenagers who handle the afternoons while I'm over at the surf shop, but it's the morning baking where I've needed the most help.

The problem, though, is Meg hasn't been shy about making her interest known. I've got six years on her, so we never ran in the same circles, but she seems to have decided that now that she's firmly an adult, we're a perfect pairing. The age difference alone is enough to keep me wary, but I haven't done much dating during the last decade. I'm not about to change that now just because a twenty-two-year-old keeps giving me bedroom eyes.

I think if Meg knew my breakfast this morning was the rest of last night's dinner, she wouldn't be so keen on pushing our relationship to be more than boss and employee.

"How are the sticky buns coming?" I ask, hoping to subtly keep her attention on the pastries and off my bare chest.

Meg lets out a little sigh and glances at the oven behind her. "Almost done. Are you okay to handle the cookies? I need to get this bread finished."

"Yes," I say. We both know I'm being overconfident. I still have no idea why my uncle left me his bakery, considering I rarely spent any time here growing up, but I suppose he had no other options. Besides, he'd only been fifty-five. No one expected him to go so soon. Not even him.

Glancing at my watch and wincing when I realize how late I am, I grab Uncle Bill's recipe book and flip to the double fudge cookie recipe, which will be the flavor of the day. Uncle Bill used to make all kinds of cookies every day, often experimenting with something new, but I'm lucky if I get through two or three flavors in a morning before I have to head to the other side of the boardwalk and open the surf shop where I'll spend the rest of the day until the sun goes down—and then start it all over again the next day.

I'm drowning, just like Prince Harry the llama, only I don't have someone to jump in and save me.

Meg clears her throat and nods toward my shirtless body. "At least put on an apron?" she suggests, though she seems reluctant about saying anything.

I'm not about to spend several hours in this kitchen in nothing but an apron, especially with my jeans hanging low on my hips because they're still soaking wet. Tossing my wet shirt into the corner of the kitchen that serves as an office, I make my way to the front of the bakery to see if there are any extra-large shirts left amongst the Kingston's Bakery merchandise. I was supposed to put in an order for more two weeks ago, but...

It's one thing on an enormous list of things I need to do before summer officially hits next week and, quite frankly, it's my lowest priority.

The lobby is almost empty outside of a couple of locals who have already claimed their usual spots despite the fact that we don't open for another hour. As always, Mrs. Vanderman is reading the local newspaper on her phone with a font so large that only one or two words fit on a line. Gary and Carl, two fishermen of indeterminate age, have set up their daily game of Battleship over by the window. It looks like Carl put on a fresh pot of coffee, and I smile as I silently make my way to the far corner by the registers, where our limited supply of t-shirts and mugs sit in their sad display.

The logo design—the words "Kingston's Bakery" overlaid on a crudely drawn muffin—hasn't changed in thirty years and is, quite frankly, pathetic. But it's Uncle Bill's. He built this place from the ground up and turned it into a Willow Cove favorite. When the tourists come flooding in for the summer every year, they always become regular customers while they're here, and I'm dreading how some people will react when they learn Bill died two months ago. He was the heart and soul of this place, a bright spot in everyone's life no matter how short a time he was a part of it.

Kingston's isn't the same without him. And not just because I'm a terrible baker. This place doesn't have the life it used to, and I'm not sure it ever will. Without Uncle Bill's optimism and broad smiles, the bakery is slowly dying right alongside my energy levels. And maybe my will to live.

The bell over the door jingles, and I quicken my search for a shirt that will fit me. The only one big enough is a bright pink tee with the logo over the left breast and a giant, low quality iron-on of a sticky bun on the back. It's a 3XL, and the thought of putting it on feels like some weird metaphor for me never being able to fill the space my uncle left. I'm pretty sure Uncle Bill made this shirt himself twenty years ago and it's been sitting on the back of the shelf ever since. But it will fit and doesn't smell like wet llama, so I'll call this a win.

Even if it makes me feel all the more incompetent.

"Oh my gosh, I wish you could smell this place, Cece!" A feminine voice fills the quiet stillness of the bakery, pulling my attention behind me before I can pull the hideous shirt on. A tourist is talking to her phone, holding it in front of her face, and her voice is way too loud for such an early hour. "It's smaller than I thought, but can you imagine how cute it would look if these booths were replaced by extra tall tables?" She gestures to the booths behind her, where Gary and Carl are sitting.

Her phone is blocking my view of her face, but she looks and sounds like someone from up north, probably one of the bigger cities like D.C. or New

York. I already don't like her, especially because she ignored the sign on the door that clearly says we're closed.

This is what I get for not locking the door.

"Oo, imagine a long countertop running along that wall over there," she says, turning her back to me as she flips her camera and pans across the far wall. "And white walls with lemon accents!"

I take in the deep green color of the walls, my frown growing deeper. Who in the world does this woman think she is? Gary and Carl have stopped their game, both with matching expressions of confusion as they watch the woman continue her assessment of my bakery.

"And a giant screen over the—" She squeaks when her phone points at me in the corner, and then she drops her arms and turns a bright red, as if she hadn't realized anyone else was in the room.

Something settles heavy in my gut. Now that I've got a good look at her, she looks far more familiar than I'd like. There's no way...

"Oh," she says, eyes quickly taking me in before dropping to her feet. "I guess someone missed the 'no shirt, no shoes, no service' sign on his way in."

I tug the t-shirt over my head, not because she said something but because I feel far too exposed. If she is who I think she is, I'm going to need thick layers of armor between me and her. A thin piece of cotton isn't going to provide much protection, but it's something. "Someone missed the 'closed' sign," I say back. My words come out rough. Strained.

The woman glances behind her, first at the sign on the door and then to the three old people sitting in their spots. "A few someones," she says slowly. Then her eyes meet mine again, and I'm hit with a sharp sense of déjà vu. They're a bright shade of green that I've only seen on one person before. Her curly hair is shorter and her face is thinner, but everything else about her is familiar.

I'm tempted to look behind me, where several pictures are taped to the wall above the merchandise display. Though I force myself to keep my gaze on the woman in the center of the room, I know exactly which photo is calling to me. It's the second one from the left, third row down, and it's a picture of Uncle Bill and a fourteen-year old girl in the bakery kitchen, both of them laughing as they decorate cupcakes. She has a streak of flour on her cheek, her hair pulled back in braids like she used to do a lot.

My fingers curl into fists as the woman starts studying me the way I'm studying her. I didn't think she would ever come back.

"I was hoping to talk to Mr. Kingston," she says, taking a small step forward.

My scowl stops her from taking another. "That's impossible."

"Please? He'll want to see me."

I'm sure he would, if he were still alive. But the fact that she's here, now, and has no idea that Uncle Bill is gone...well, it doesn't bode well for me. She hasn't recognized me yet, but she will.

I fold my arms. "We're closed," I say sharply. Gary and Carl give each other pointed glances, and Mrs. Vanderman looks like she badly wants to interrupt this exchange, but the three of them keep silent. "You can come back later if you really want, but it's not going to get you a meeting with Bill Kingston."

The woman pouts and tucks a dark curl behind her ear, making my stomach twist into a knot. My doubts that I know exactly who she is are dwindling with every expression and gesture she makes. As if my day wasn't bad enough already... "It really won't take a long time," she says and cranes her neck, trying to see into the kitchen through the swinging door separating the lobby from the back. "I promise Bill will want—"

"Come back later."

"But I—"

"*Georgie.*" Her name tumbles off my tongue almost painfully, leaving behind the taste of acid.

The color drains from her face as her eyes take me in once more. I don't think I look that different, but it still takes a few seconds before recognition sets in. "Royal," she whispers, and I can't help but wince at her use of my first name. She's the only person who has ever really called me by my actual name.

"King," I correct and point to the door. "Later. I'll find you."

I don't move until she's gone, the bell signaling her departure, but even then my limbs feel like lead. *Georgie Carpenter is in Willow Cove.* It's like something out of a nightmare, the kind that sticks with you long after you wake up. The last time I saw her, she was looking out a plane window and disappearing into the sunset, and I was trying to figure out how I could have seen her as anything but a coward and a quitter who would so easily tear my heart to shreds without a single word.

Chapter Two

Georgie

I GUESS I SHOULD have expected to see Royal—King—when I got to Willow Cove. I knew he likely still lived here, and I knew he would be on the boardwalk at some point because that was where he spent all his time back when we were... Well, I figured it would happen before long, but I didn't expect to see him in the *bakery* of all places. He hated that place! I was sort of banking on him avoiding Kingston's until I had a chance to find my footing, even if his uncle owns the place.

After King kicks me out of Bill's bakery, I spend the morning sitting on the beach and ignoring Cecily's repeated calls. I hung up on her suddenly at the sight of a shirtless King, and she hasn't left me alone since. But I don't think I'll be able to explain why I've been off balance ever since realizing that the well-toned man of a man showing off his muscly torso in the bakery this morning was *Royal Kingston*.

My best friend doesn't know King exists, and I'd like to keep it that way. Some things are better left in the past, and King is the source of my biggest regrets. A girl doesn't easily talk about the man she left behind in the worst possible way.

Goodness, but I forgot how warm it can get in South Carolina, and more than likely my morning on the beach is going to leave me red and tender, but there's really nowhere else for me to go. Willow Cove is small on a good day, and when I spent summers here as a kid, I was always either in the bakery with Bill or on the beach with King. The bakery isn't an option, so the beach it is.

I didn't exactly make a plan before I came here, so I don't have a place to stay. Nor can I easily afford a room in the Coralberry Cottages after draining my checking account to pay for the gas to make the drive from New York and rolling into town on fumes.

If Bill can't help me, I'm not sure what I'm going to do. This journey was a Hail Mary.

It's almost noon before King finds me watching the waves from the end of the boardwalk, and I'm genuinely surprised he actually came. With the way he glared at me—not that I can blame him—I expected to be waiting on the boardwalk until his uncle closed the bakery later this afternoon.

King rests his elbows on the railing about a foot from me without a word, his eyes on the ocean and his jaw tight. And wow, does he have a jaw. The last time I saw this man, he was a gangly teenager with barely a sign of facial hair, and the man next to me is...not that.

He's still got his mop of dark hair, though he's cut it slightly shorter on the sides so it doesn't curl over his ears anymore, and his brown eyes are as bottomless as ever. His face isn't as round as it used to be, full of angles and edges, and scruff lines his cheeks in a way it never did before. He looks like someone took hold of his eighteen-year-old self and, like clay, molded him into a man.

I gotta admit, they did a good job on him. I always thought he was cute, but grown-up Royal Kingston is certifiably gorgeous.

"Are you done?" he growls, glancing at me from the corner of his eye.

My face flames. "Can I talk to Bill now?"

"No."

"I get that you're not happy to see me, King, but I really need to talk to him."

"Why?" He finally looks at me, turning his head to give me a full view of his face. Now that I'm seeing him in the sunlight, he looks tired. Haggard. Like he hasn't had a good night's sleep in weeks. "Why are you so desperate to talk to Uncle Bill?"

I know him well enough to know that he's not going to do anything until he gets an answer; this man can be almost as stubborn as me. But I'm not used to this hardened version of him, and the truth would be a whole lot easier to admit if he was still the happy-go-lucky guy I used to know.

Taking a deep breath, I grip the strap of my purse and shift my eyes to the gentle waves as they wash in. "I need a job." That's greatly understating it, but it's about all I can manage right now.

"So you came to a town of three thousand people?" He lets out a short bark of a laugh. "Smart move."

"Bill always said there would be room for me at the bakery."

"New York wasn't quaint enough for you?"

A little gasp escapes me, though I shouldn't be surprised. Bill must have told him where I ended up, and I can't help but wonder how much King knows about my life over the last ten years. Does he know about my boyfriend dumping me on national television? I really hope not.

Frustration builds inside me, leaving me feeling buzzy and unsettled. There's petty, and then there's King holding a grudge for a decade.

"Look," I say, turning to face him and hoping I can come across as confident when I feel anything but. "My job in New York took a turn I wasn't equipped to take, and I always loved my summers at Kingston's. Willow Cove felt like a good place to land until I figure out what my next move is."

"Temporary," he mutters and stands up straight so he can put his hands in his pockets. The gesture makes his arms look enormous and accentuates his broad chest. "Look, Georgie, I don't know what you were hoping to find on this little adventure of yours, but you and I both know you're not meant for a place like this."

There's a lot of undercurrent in his words, things he probably won't say out loud even though he likely wants to.

I sigh. "I don't have a lot of choices right now, King." Or any choices, really. I just spent the last two weeks trying to find a place for me that wasn't bottom rung, and I came up empty. Turns out, when you're tossed out of a successful company without warning, people tend to assume the worst of you. "Can I please just explain things to Bill?"

Clenching his jaw, he looks down the boardwalk, which has slowly started to fill with more people. It's not quite summer, so Willow Cove isn't swarming with tourists yet, but it will be. And soon. Bill will need all the help he can get.

"You can't talk to Bill," he says slowly.

My face heats again, this time with anger. "Seriously? You can't just—"

"He died, Georgie. Two months ago."

All of my fight leaves in a whoosh of air, leaving me dizzy enough that I have to grip the boardwalk railing. "What? He's gone?" Disbelief shoots through me as I try to understand. Bill wasn't even that old, and he was always so lively. Getting up early in the morning to bake, spending the afternoons out in the surf, going for runs in the evenings... He can't be gone. He was a staple of this town and one of my most favorite people in the world, which suddenly feels a lot less bright.

What am I going to do now? He was the first person who made me believe I could forge my own path in life instead of accepting whatever plan others expected of me. He made me feel strong and confident and brave.

I need his pride in me more than ever right now, but all I have now is sorrow knowing I'll never get the chance to talk to him again or even thank him again for looking out for me all these years. His phone calls over the years were sometimes the only thing that kept me going.

With a little grunt, King turns and starts heading back down the boardwalk.

"Wait," I gasp, "where are you going?" He can't drop something like that on me and walk away! It's hard enough to process Bill being gone, but King's uncle was my only chance at taking the next step in my career unless I want to start back at the beginning. I don't know if I have another ten years in me just to get back to a point where I can be proud of something I've built with my own talents.

King doesn't look back. "I'm going to work, Georgie. Some of us have jobs."

"But you're going in the wrong direction." The bakery is the other way.

Though he glances back, he doesn't say anything else as he continues down the wooden walkway that makes up Coral Berry Boardwalk. It's the biggest tourist destination in Willow Cove outside of the many islands off the coast that can be explored by boat or floatplane. The boardwalk looks so familiar but so different at the same time, and my brain is having a hard time reconciling the Willow Cove of ten years ago with the one I'm in now. I think a part of me expected it to be the same as it was when I left.

Taking a set of stairs down to the beach, King doesn't stop walking until he hits the old surf shop where he used to work. Only, it's not so old now. As I approach, everything looks like it's only a few years old instead of falling apart. It's actually a warm and welcoming place—King always thought that about the old shack as well. He always said the surf shack was his second home, a place where people could be brave and become something they'd never been before. A sentiment he learned from Bill.

"I can't believe you still work here," I breathe, watching him open the big window and prop the double doors open to let the breeze in. "Old Man Skewer must be eighty years old by now."

"He's also dead," King replies as he flips on the lights. Jack Johnson starts playing overhead, and he grabs a navy shirt from one of the racks and switches out the bright pink one he was wearing before. This one is a lot more flattering than the other, clinging to his skin like a glove. "Passed nine years ago."

"Oh." Then I see the logo on his shirt and the colorful words "King's Surf Shop" front and center. "You own the place now."

He nods once. "Bought it before Skewer died."

"How?" He would have only been nineteen at the time.

Letting out a bone-weary sigh, he folds his arms and pins me with a sharp look.

I do my best not to wither. "I'm guessing you own the bakery now too?"

Before he can answer, though I'm not sure he would have said anything, his eyes jump to the open doors as a customer walks in, wide-eyed and eager.

"Whoa, look at this place! This is legit!"

King plasters on a smile and greets the customer with all the warmth he's failed to give me this morning.

I shuffle over to the corner with all the t-shirts, looking at the many designs lined up along the wall. One of them, with its palm tree and stick-figure person with a surfboard, looks like it was drawn by a little kid, and it's instantly my favorite. It looks like it's a crowd favorite as well, as it has the lowest inventory out of all of them. It has a very King feel to it.

As surprised as I was to see him in the bakery this morning, I'm not surprised that he took over the surf shop. He's always been happiest on the water, and he started teaching surf lessons for Old Man Skewer when he was thirteen. King's a natural born teacher, and I can't help but picture him now, straddling a board in a form-fitting wetsuit with a broad smile on his face as he helps other people find joy in riding the waves.

It's strange, but I've missed his smile more than anything over the years. Like Bill, he has—or maybe *had*—the kind of smile that could brighten even the gloomiest of days.

Trying not to get lost in thoughts of what could have been, I lean my hand on the t-shirt display, but it collapses under my weight and sends me tumbling to the floor. I shriek, protecting my head from the avalanche of wood shelves and polyester shirts, but it's over in three seconds flat.

I might just stay here. If the humiliation doesn't kill me, King probably will.

"Georgie?" His voice is muffled through all the shirts.

"I'm fine," I squeak back.

"You need some help?"

"Nope."

"Okay then."

I feel his footsteps through the floorboards. He's literally walking away from me! Groaning, I lift myself onto my elbows and start army-crawling free, muttering curses under my breath. I'm pretty sure the last decade used up all the good fortune for my lifetime, leaving me with nothing but tragedy from now on.

And to think, at one point I thought I was pretty lucky in life. I had a great apartment, a promising career, a loving boyfriend...

Now I have none of those things and nowhere to go, and the only man who might help is about as likely to come to my aid as he is to give up surfing.

By the time I get free, King is ringing up his customer and chatting away like the carefree people-person I remember. Sitting myself on the floor, I start grabbing shirts to refold. He was right when he questioned my decision to come here. Outside of the summer season, Willow Cove is a sleepy little town with not a lot going on. It's not like Manhattan, where my days were full to the brim. I spent all my summers as a teen here with my parents as they did marine research for the university they worked for, but when I turned eighteen, I was so excited to go anywhere that wasn't here.

Graduating high school opened up the world to me, and New York was this big, magical place with endless opportunity. I was lucky to find my first job in a bakery a block from Central Park, even luckier a few years later to be working on a day when a network exec was looking for fresh talent. She put me in a competition I wasn't qualified for, and by some miracle I made it to the top three and met Lane. He was cute, and his passion for baking was intoxicating.

After the competition wrapped up, he asked me out. We bonded over puff pastry and fondant, and he shared my dreams of owning my own bakery, suggesting we make one together. We were already suited romantically, and he thought we would be great together professionally as well.

I helped him build a baking empire, complete with a TV show and franchises, and he and I were going to take on the world. At least, we were until he decided out of the blue that he wanted to take it on without me. Nothing like a little live television to spice up a breakup, am I right? It's not like I poured my soul into our franchise...

"And then I took her on a floatplane at sunset," King says, his deep voice cutting through my reverie.

"That sounds incredible!" the customer replies, apparently enthralled.

I'm probably not allowed to be jealous of whichever woman got such a romantic date with King, but I am. He did that with me, once upon a time, and he has always been a romantic. Definitely not the type of guy to stage a public breakup for the views. For all his gruffness this morning, I can still confidently say that King would never humiliate me, no matter how hurt and angry he might be.

"We ended up on this tiny little island right as the sun was setting," King continues, "and since I'd been carrying the ring in my pocket for weeks, I figured that was as good a time as any."

I gasp, my stomach doing a flip. The woman I'm jealous of is me!

The man on the other side of the counter whistles low. "I'm not sure I can top that."

"Oh, you can." King's eyes meet mine, his expression falsely nonchalant. "See, when I asked her to marry me, she panicked."

"No!"

"Yes. And I get it. The proposal came out of nowhere. She needed time to process. But for her, that meant forcing the pilot to fly her back to Willow Cove without me."

"Wait, she left you on the island?"

King nods, still looking right at me. "The plane came back for me later that night, but not until after she packed up and left town."

"For how long?"

"About ten years."

The man laughs uncomfortably. "That's rough. Maybe I'll keep my proposal nice and simple. Nothing that'll scare her off."

"That's a great idea. And I'm sure you'll have better luck than I did. Thanks for coming to King's Surf Shop!" King smiles and waves as the guy heads out. The instant he's gone, King's smile drops and his eyes jump to me.

I try not to scowl at him, but I'm pretty sure my attempts get lost in the feelings of guilt that bubble up. I already spent plenty of time feeling guilty over the way I left things, and I don't need more of it now when I'm still reeling from the news that Bill died. "That was a fun story," I grumble.

"That was a true story."

"I didn't think Coop would take that long to go back for you."

"Yep, that makes it all better." He comes over and starts lifting all the wood plank shelves, popping them back into place with ease. "You really shouldn't be back here, Georgie."

He's probably right. "I had nowhere else to go."

"What about your parents?"

I keep my eyes on the shirt I'm folding. "You know I love my parents, but if I go crawling back to them, they'll smother me with love and pie and try to set me up with some accountant who will provide me with a cushy, quiet life."

"The horror!"

I ball up a shirt and throw it at him, though I can't blame him for his sarcasm. He lost both his parents before he turned fifteen, so I really shouldn't complain that I have both of mine. "I thought I might find a fresh start in Willow Cove, you know? Away from it all."

The thought makes me tired. All the hard work of the last ten years of my life was taken away from me in an instant, leaving me craving something stable and familiar, something that wouldn't make me a burden to someone else. Something like Kingston's, where I always felt like I was a part of something magical. Thoughts of that bakery were the only thing that kept me sane the last couple of weeks, knowing I would have a soft place to land as everything in New York crumbled.

I *could* go back to my parents' house, but now that they're both retired, there's only so much they can do to help me get back on my feet. Being biology professors didn't exactly set them up with wealth, so I'm going to have to rely on myself going forward. I haven't even told them yet that I had to leave New York because they would probably try to give me a chunk of their limited retirement fund.

To my surprise, King stops rebuilding his shelves and sits on the floor next to me. Though he keeps his gaze down at the shirts in front of him, I know his focus is really on me. "Bill talked about you all the time, you know."

I smile, wishing he would look at me. "I bet you hated that."

"With a passion. He was always proud of you."

I sense a 'but' in there, but I'm too afraid to ask. Too bad for me, King keeps talking.

"But I don't know what kind of fresh start you'll find in a place like this. Willow Cove is too small for a big city girl like you."

He's probably right, but summer is coming quickly. This town gets crazy in the summer. Or, it used to. Maybe all that has changed over the last decade. "Like I said, it would just be temporary."

Actually, *he's* the one who said that, and if I had my way, it wouldn't be temporary at all. At least, I would stay long enough to get the bakery thriving and under the right manager. That could take months, maybe even a year, and then I would hang on to it and use the profits to start something else in a bigger city. I made a whole plan as I drove down here.

"I was really hoping to take over the bakery for Bill," I say carefully. Something tells me I'm going to have to tread carefully here.

His dark eyes search my face for a moment. "Sorry you wasted a trip."

"I'll buy it from you." Those words jump from my mouth before I can hold them back. *Buy* the bakery? With what? My savings account is enough to keep me fed for maybe a year, but that's about it. I still need to find health insurance and a place to live, neither of which will come cheaply. I was banking on the bakery being a gift.

Yeah, I had an awesome job within a multi-million-dollar company, but all my money went to my apartment and to the lifestyle I adopted alongside Lane. I never thought I would lose it all.

King watches me for a beat, studying me intently before he folds his arms. "You want to buy Uncle Bill's bakery?"

No. "Yes." *Shut up, Georgie!* "I know you don't want it."

"How do you know?"

"You always hated that bakery. You complained about it every day."

"A decade ago."

Okay, so maybe he has a point, but I can't imagine this man has changed *that* much over the last ten years. He might be grown up and manly now, but I'd bet the old Royal Kingston is still in there. The one who never failed to get so annoyed when I'd spend all day with Bill at the bakery and then shut up when I offered him a snickerdoodle or a cherry tartlet fresh out of the oven. I've always been able to persuade King to do things; I just need to find the right motivation.

"Well?" I reach forward and take hold of his hand. I try not to let it hurt too much when he pulls away without hesitation. "It might take me a day or two to get the loan figured out, but I'll buy it and take it off your hands. I get the bakery, you get a bunch of money. Win win."

He's considering it. I know he is. King could never resist a quick buck, and that bakery is probably worth a decent amount. Granted, I have no idea if I could get a loan, but that won't stop me from—

"I can't." King pushes up to his feet, leaving me in a heap on the floor. "Can't sell it to you, Georgie. It's a family legacy."

I jump up as well, even though I've folded maybe ten shirts in total, which is nothing compared to the pile still waiting. This is more important. "Are you kidding me? No one loved that bakery as much as I did. Is this because I refused your proposal?"

"Did you refuse? I remember you saying a whole lot of nothing." He moves to the other side of the store and grabs a surfboard from the rack where they're all lined up.

Again, he's right, and we should probably talk about the whole proposal thing instead of arguing about the bakery, but my mind is fixated on this and won't let me stop pushing. "King, please. I'll pay more than it's worth."

"Doesn't matter."

I follow him out the door and watch as he rests the board against the outside of the shop like some sort of display. "Come on."

"No, I..." He grits his teeth, folding his arms once more as he turns to face me. "I literally can't sell you the bakery. Or even give it to you. Uncle Bill did something weird with his will, and the bakery has to stay in the family."

"Oh." The fight drains out of me as I consider that. Is that even a thing someone can do? I don't know enough about law to really question it, but King seems genuine. "That seems a little..." Stupid. That's what it is.

King shrugs. "It's Uncle Bill. What did you expect?"

I expected him to leave me the bakery, like he always said he would, but I keep that to myself. He probably decided I was thriving up in New York and didn't need it. After all, I never gave him a reason to believe otherwise.

"I could hire you to run the place," King says, but before I can even consider the idea, he cringes. "I can't afford you. Not without dipping into my profits from the surf shack, and..." His eyes roll over me. "Not doing that. You're too fancy."

I can't decide if his assessment of me is a compliment or an insult. "I can lower my salary expectations." But even as I say that, my mind starts running through all the updates the bakery needs to be successful. I'm pretty sure the salary from working a whole Willow Cove tourist summer would barely be enough to cover the costs of the badly needed renovations. There's no way I could afford making those changes unless I'm actually owning the place and have the profits at my disposal.

King narrows his eyes. Back when we were dating, he had this habit of reading my mind. It was always cute and endearing, but right now I don't like the way he seems to be seeing the dollar signs running through my head.

"Can't you find some sort of loophole?" I ask weakly.

He huffs a laugh. "So you can change everything about Uncle Bill's bakery?"

See? Mind reader. I grimace. "I wouldn't change *everything*."

"That's not what you said to your friend this morning." Rolling his eyes, he heads back inside and drops down to continue folding the shirts I left behind.

I'm not making myself sound great. I know that. But I spent the last year butting heads with Lane, trying to make our relationship work, until he decided our personalities clashed as much as our opinions on the best way to make buttercream. He was too hard-headed to listen to my ideas, and I endured it because I thought our relationship, both romantic and professional, was worth the concessions. It clearly wasn't.

He not only dumped me on TV but also strong-armed me out of the bakery franchise on the technicality that it's his name on the ownership documents.

I need this. Working with Bill at Kingston's over the summer after I turned thirteen was the first time I ever felt like I had any sort of say in my life. One, my parents were busy with their research and didn't ask how I spent my days when we were in Willow Cove, so they had no idea I was in Bill's kitchen. And two, baking was something I was good at. Something that brought excitement to my life. The rest of the year was all about school and grades, but summer?

I took that passion and did everything I could to make a career out of it, and Lane took it all away in a moment, pulling the rug out from under me.

No one can plan for something like that.

King and I spend the next few minutes folding shirts in silence, the air thick with tension. I'm still not completely over the shock of seeing full-blown adult King, and I'm sure he wasn't planning on running into me, of all people. I don't know what to do now or where to go, and I hate that. I like having a plan. A direction. This compass-less life I've been living the last couple of weeks has left me feeling like I'm drifting out to sea.

And I'm terrified of the ocean.

"I wish there was a way to help you," King says after a while. It seems to take a lot out of him to speak the words out loud, but his mama raised him to be a good man. Now that we've settled a bit, it's obvious that that side of him is coming out. "But Uncle Bill was clear in his will. It has to stay with the Kingstons."

"But you're the only..." My words trail off as the realization hits me way later than it should have. He's the only Kingston left. First his dad, then his mom, and now Bill...

King is entirely alone.

He looks up and meets my gaze. There's sadness in his expression, but it's not like my epiphany is news to him. He knows very well that he's alone, and he almost seems to be okay with it. I'm not sure if I believe him. I knew him when his mom died, and I know how deeply he feels things. Losing Bill must have hurt him so much.

"Sorry," I whisper.

He shrugs. "If I could give you the bakery, I would, but short of adopting you into the family, I don't—"

"That's it!" I accidentally toss a shirt at him again because of the idea that just popped into my head.

He catches it, nothing but confusion in his face. "What? Adopt you? Last I checked, you're a grown woman with two very much alive parents, Georgie."

Maybe there's a way we can both win here, at least temporarily. He wouldn't have to be so alone for a while. "Not adopt, per se, but similar. It's a way to get me into the Kingston family."

He's still not getting it, one thick eyebrow high on his forehead as he stares at me like I'm talking crazy.

I *am* talking crazy. Absolutely. But it might be my best option, and I don't have a lot of those.

I see the exact moment it clicks, and while I expected him to dislike the idea, I hoped for better than complete and utter disgust. His eyebrows shoot down, his jaw clenches, and for half a second he looks like he might throw up.

Then his features soften as he calms. Considers. And I hold my breath as he opens his mouth to say, "Absolutely not. If you wanted to marry me, you should have done that ten years ago. Time for you to leave."

Chapter Three

King

SHE DOESN'T LEAVE. NOT that I expected her to. But I hoped. Oh, how I hoped.

Getting to my feet, I shove t-shirts anywhere they'll fit and move to the other side of the counter to put something between me and Georgie.

As I knew she would, Georgie follows, rambling as she goes. "Okay, but it would work! Just listen. If we get married, I'll technically be family, and then you could sell me the bakery. It'll be like cheating the dumb system, and we don't even have to do anything other than get the marriage license to make it all legal. I would be a Kingston, and you wouldn't be alone, and everyone wins. We get married, transfer the bakery to me, and then we get divorced. Simple!"

There is nothing simple about it. "You want to *get married* so you can buy a bakery. Do you have any idea how crazy that sounds?"

"People get married for far less."

"Ha!"

Today has been one nightmare after another, and it's not even one o'clock. It'd be really nice if I could wake up and discover it's one in the *morning* and I still have a couple hours to sleep before I have to be at the bakery. And hopefully then I wouldn't burn several batches of cookies because I'm so distracted by Georgie's sudden appearance that I can't concentrate on anything right now. It's like my mind is stuck inside a wave that won't stop rolling. Everything is foggy, and I've got a monster headache that popped up when I pulled yet another blackened batch of cookies out of the oven two hours ago.

Meg looked like she was reconsidering her interest in me by that point, which isn't exactly a bad thing. Not having cookies to sell *is* a bad thing, and a few of the locals weren't pleased when they stopped by and only had lumpy muffins to choose from. I've been lucky that they're still willing to show up every day even though Meg and I are nowhere close to Bill's equals in the kitchen, but today may have driven them all off.

My stomach churns thinking about the bakery falling to ruin because I can't keep it alive.

"C'mon, King. Just a marriage of convenience, on paper only, no strings attached. I get the bakery, and you don't have to watch it fall apart and die because you're juggling two businesses. This could work."

"Maybe," I reluctantly agree. It's like she's reading my mind, which is terrifying. "But that doesn't mean I think it's a good idea." After today's disaster of a morning, I wouldn't mind selling the bakery and getting some space to breathe, even if selling feels like I'm stomping on Uncle Bill's grave. I highly doubt Georgie can afford it, based on the look in her eyes when she first offered, but even if she could...

I'm not sure I could handle what she's suggesting.

Sure, I haven't seen this woman in a decade, but every minute I spend with her seems to hit me with a new memory. Another little tidbit about her that I worked so hard to forget. It's not easy getting over a heartache as deep as mine, and apparently I didn't do as good a job of forgetting her as I thought.

I can't look at her without feeling like I'm being punched in the gut. The thought of being anywhere near her, let alone *married* to her, is making me nauseous and dizzy.

But how else am I going to keep the bakery going?

She leans her elbows on the countertop, fixing those big green eyes on me in a way that always used to get me to agree to anything she wanted. Even before we started dating and were just summer friends, she had a knack for getting me to jump into whatever idea popped into her head. Her passion and enthusiasm were what drew me to her in the first place, and she's brimming with excitement the same way she used to. "King." She punctuates my name with a tiny smile. "Please. I'm desperate here, and I just want something to go right in my life for once."

You and me both. Honestly, my life was pretty good up until Uncle Bill got sick. I had the surf shop and the house I've been renovating for myself, and I was even thinking of taking some trips to get myself outside of the bubble that is Willow Cove. Maybe start dating again.

If the sheen of sweat on the back of my neck is any indication, I'm so not ready for dating if I'm still this hot and bothered by seeing Georgie Carpenter.

Selling the bakery to Georgie would cut my problems in half, but deep down I know it wouldn't last. *She* won't last. I'll be giving up the last ties I have to my family, and she'll bulldoze her way through to turn it into something else before she rushes off to do the next thing, leaving me completely alone. Uncle Bill has only been gone for two months, and already it feels like he's disappearing every time I step into that bakery. The man raised me after I lost my mom at fourteen, and I can't repay him by handing over the thing he loved most to someone who won't respect it.

I fold my arms, swallowing the thick emotion that has decided to lodge itself in my throat. "I can't marry you, Georgie."

Something shifts in her expression as she studies me. "You already have someone in your life," she guesses.

I'm pretty sure she knows how wrong she is. Now that Uncle Bill is gone, I have no one. No one except Prince Harry, the pool-loving llama. "I wish I could help you, but—"

"I get it." Standing up straight, she looks around the shop in a way that tells me she's not seeing any of it. Georgie has always had this habit of imagining the future, overthinking her current situation and envisioning the path she's on. Usually with all the ways things could go wrong. She tries to control every situation so she doesn't end up disappointed or hurt.

She got the same look when I proposed, and I immediately knew I was going to lose her, even before she ran. Or flew, technically. I can't go through that again.

Before I can give her another pathetic argument, someone walks into the shop. "Hi," the customer says, his eyes full of excitement. "I signed up for a surfing lesson this afternoon?"

He's early, but I prefer that to being late. Still, I can't leave the shop until my employee Brody gets here to handle any sales. He should arrive any minute, so I'll kill some time and chat.

"You must be Sean." Putting on a smile, I wave a greeting to my new pupil, but the shop phone starts ringing. *What now?* "Excuse me a second, will you?" I answer the phone, forcing some extra cheer into my voice. "King's Surf Shop, how can I—"

"King!" Meg's voice sounds frantic. "Any chance you can come back?"

I frown. "What's going on?"

"Tour bus."

I swear under my breath and look up at the eager student. This is my first lesson of the season, and I really need to start off on the right foot. "I can't," I tell Meg, hating every word. "The bus shouldn't be around for long, so—"

"It's full of *old people*, King, and apparently they planned this whole stop around coming to Kingston's."

I swear again, my stomach twisting into a knot. Nausea keeps building in my gut, and I'm starting to think it's not all from Georgie's visit. My heart is beating way too fast, and there's a sort of ringing in my ears that is making it hard to hear

Meg as she regales me with the full scope of what she's dealing with at the bakery. The geriatric crowd tends to leave the most scathing reviews, and the selection of goods is already slim as it is.

My eyes jump to Georgie, who watches me with thinly veiled interest in her eyes. Bile rises in my throat, and I have the sudden realization that I only have a few precious seconds before crap hits the fan. Or vomit hits the floor, technically speaking. My stomach is positively roiling.

"Hold down the fort for a few minutes," I tell Meg and hang up. Then I look at Sean and grimace. "Sorry, man, but something has come up, and I'm going to have to cancel your lesson. I'll give you a refund, or we can reschedule for tomorrow."

Thankfully, Sean doesn't seem too disappointed as he reschedules for tomorrow afternoon, wishing me luck with whatever came up.

The moment he's gone, I turn to Georgie. She's not saying anything out loud, but her smirk is the same one she always got when she issued a challenge. And I could never resist one of her challenges. I don't know what it is about her, but she gets under my skin in the most irritating way and makes me feel like I need to match her step for step. She's like an addiction I just can't shake.

Cursing again, I let out a groan and fold my arms. "I'll do it." I'm going to regret this, but now is not the time for overthinking. If I'm not careful and get her some real help as soon as possible, Meg will quit and leave me even worse for wear, and I already know I won't be any help to anyone in a moment. Georgie is great at tackling tough situations. At least, I'm hoping she still is.

Georgie's eyebrows fly high. "You'll do what?"

"You wanna get married, let's get married. You can have the bakery. I don't—" My words are drowned out by my stomach deciding to do a double backflip. I barely make it to the garbage in time to unload the entirety of my leftover dinner breakfast, which does nothing to soothe the rolling sensation in my gut. Groaning, I grip the edges of the can as I wait for the world to stop spinning.

"King, are you okay?" Georgie's question precedes her hand on my shoulder. Her touch is simultaneously burning hot and freezing cold. "Oh wow, you're hot."

"Under any other circumstances I would thank you for the compliment." I moan, willing my legs to keep working instead of giving out beneath me, like they're threatening to do. Whatever this is, it sucks. Probably food poisoning, but it feels worse than that. I feel like my body is trying to turn itself inside out.

"King, you need to go home."

"Yeah," I agree, but it's not like the world is going to pause while I crawl my way back to my truck. And I can barely stomach the idea of driving all the way home when I can barely hold myself upright. "Can you..." I heave again, wondering how there's anything left after the first time.

Georgie puts her arm around me. "I can help you get home, yes."

"No."

"What?"

"The..." I swallow and sink to the floor, tempted to lie down but knowing I'll never get back up if I do. "The bakery. If you want the bakery, you need to go help. Right now."

I'm vaguely aware of her face next to mine as she crouches, but I can't keep my eyes open as my stomach continues to churn. "But what about you?" she says. "I can't just leave you like this."

"You've left me with worse."

She breathes in sharply, and then she wraps my arm around her shoulders. "Okay, big guy. You're coming with me."

I'm too tired and nauseous to argue, as much as I want to. "Where?"

Grunting as she struggles to her feet without much help from me, she doesn't say anything until we're walking. Guess I'll have to trust that Brody will get to the shop soon and things will be fine until he does.

"You can lie down in the back of the bakery," Georgie says when we hit the sand. "You probably shouldn't be alone like this. Do you need an ambulance?"

Like I can afford that? I'm running two businesses, one of which is barely staying afloat and the other which only sees significant profits during a few months of the year. I groan.

"I'll take that as a no."

The journey down the boardwalk is agony, and I have to stop at two different garbage cans before we finally make it to Kingston's. Georgie smartly brings me around back, given the sheer number of elderly customers in the lobby that I can smell more than I can see. I've never hated floral perfume more than I do right now, and it nearly triggers another heave, though at this point there's nothing left.

Georgie deposits me underneath the desk in the corner, giving me an apron as a pillow and a mixing bowl in case my stomach magically finds more to empty, and then she heads up front like she owns the place.

And as I curl up in a ball and hope whatever this is passes quickly, I can't help but think about how Georgie *will* own this place because I just agreed to give it to her. Worse than that, I just agreed to *marry her*. And while I can't claim to be the best of men, I have always been a man of my word.

This marriage will only last long enough for me to transfer the bakery to Georgie's name, but no matter how short it is, it's going to be...

I grab the mixing bowl and heave again. *That*. It's going to be that.

Chapter Four

Georgie

I LIKE MEG. SHE has a no-nonsense attitude about her, and though she was skeptical at first when I appeared out of nowhere and offered to help, she warmed up to me as soon as I showed her the photo of me and Bill from when I was a kid. She liked me even more when I moved to the kitchen and started making cookies as quickly as I could to help appease the never-ending line of senior citizens who had apparently heard about the bakery on a travel blog and each were determined to have a taste.

Being in a kitchen again, without a dozen cameras in my face, feels nice. More than nice. I feel like myself again instead of an extension of Lane, and there's something warm and familiar about Bill's kitchen. It's badly out of date and needs a million upgrades, but this is where I spent my summers until I graduated high school, and I've missed this place.

I can already feel all my anxieties from being aimless melting away.

It's that feeling that I cling to as thoughts about my proposal run through my head nonstop. *I asked King to marry me.* Which is insane on so many levels. But no matter how many times I run through my options, I can't think of another way to make it work because the ovens need to be replaced and the floors are perpetually sticky and the point-of-sale system is so old that it takes way too long to do any transactions. If I'm going to save this bakery, I need money to fix it. Money I don't have but the bakery does.

I don't stop baking cookies until two teenage girls show up to relieve Meg, and she tells me I can take King home, glancing at him while she does. He's been snoring softly for a couple of hours now and looks a whole lot better than he did when we left the surf shop. I'm assuming he got hit with food poisoning, but it came on so violently that I'm genuinely worried he has a stomach bug or something. I do need to get him home, though I have no idea where that is. Last time I was here, he lived with Bill, but I wouldn't be surprised if his housing situation has changed along with everything else.

After taking the last batch of cookies out of the oven, I clean up my workstation and then crouch beside King, who is still a bit pale and sweaty. I nudge his shoulder. "You alive down there?"

He jolts awake, taking a few seconds to focus on me. "Georgie," he rasps. "Where…" He looks around the bakery and then winces. "What time is it?"

"Almost four."

He swears under his breath and starts trying to sit up. He's not doing a good job of it; he looks completely spent, and I'm wondering if it's all because of the illness. He looked tired before all this came on. "I need to get back to the shop."

I grab his arm and help him sit up, though I stop him from standing. "You need to take it slow, big guy. Meg called the surf shop and talked to someone."

"Brody. Hopefully." He runs a hand down his face and grimaces, but then something shifts in his expression. "Do I smell snickerdoodles?"

I laugh. "I don't think a cookie is a good idea right now, King."

Turning a bit green, he nods slowly. "I agree. I meant…" His eyes meet mine. "You baked them?"

"There was a serious lack of product on your shelves. Someone had to feed the masses."

He grits his teeth and then grabs hold of the folding desk chair, using it to lift himself to his feet. His muscles strain as he moves, easy to see because of the way his sweat-soaked shirt clings to his body, and I still can't comprehend how the boy I knew turned into *this*. King is the epitome of tall, dark, and handsome, and it's a miracle no one has locked him down yet. I really figured he would be married with several kids by this point, given how excited he was about the whole idea of starting a family.

My stomach does a little flip, and I almost hope it's the same bug that got to him. Otherwise, this uncomfortable feeling is guilt, and that feels like a bad emotion to have going into a marriage.

Honestly, I'm not sure King even realizes that he agreed to my harebrained idea.

"Let me help you home," I say, hoping we can have a conversation about my proposal when we're not in danger of being overheard by sweet and bubbly seventeen-year-olds.

King grumbles something, probably telling me that he doesn't need my help, but his legs nearly give out halfway to the door and he stops. Looks back at me. Nods.

I wrap his arm around my shoulders like before and follow his directions to his truck, and when he squints at the big vehicle, I ask him for his keys and bring him to the passenger seat. I'll have to come back for my car at some point, though I don't like the idea of leaving it in the boardwalk parking lot for too long. Most of my possessions are in that car, which reminds me that I still don't have a place to stay tonight.

It might be too much to hope that King will let me camp out in his guest bedroom, assuming he even has one. I'm imagining him in a bachelor pad with nothing but a pullout couch and a miniscule kitchen.

"Where am I going?" I ask when King eventually manages to get his seatbelt on. He looks like he might fall asleep before I even turn the key.

"South," he mumbles and then holds out his hand. I'm not sure what he wants, and I'm certainly not going to hold his hand. I might be willing to marry this guy, but it'll be on paper only. He sighs. "Your phone, Georgie."

"Oh."

He types in an address and then slumps back in his seat. It isn't in the direction of Bill's house, and curiosity has me driving a little over the speed limit until I pull up outside a cute little bungalow right off the coast. It's surrounded by mature magnolia and oak trees and looks well-maintained. I don't really know what I expected, but it wasn't this.

"Thanks," King mutters and slips out of the truck. Literally. One second he's climbing out, and the next he disappears with a grunt and a thud.

Gasping, I hurry around to find him sprawled in the dirt, a look of irritation on his face. "You okay?"

"Peachy."

It takes almost five minutes to get him from the truck to the master bedroom because he's moving so slowly, and I can only hold so much of his weight without feeling like I might collapse beneath him. I don't even get a chance to look around because I'm so focused on holding him up. I am more than glad when he slumps face first onto the bed, fully clothed, and kicks off his shoes.

"Thanks," he mumbles into the mattress.

"Do you need anything?"

He simply hums.

Thinking I should get him some water, I head back down the hallway and to the kitchen at the back of the house. As soon as I get a good look, I freeze in my tracks. Light streams in through the large windows, illuminating the most luxurious kitchen I've seen outside of a TV set. It's bigger than I would have expected, with granite countertops and stainless steel appliances amidst gorgeous mahogany cabinets. A massive island sits in the center, begging to be spread with pastry dough and cookie sheets.

"And here I was thinking you didn't care about the kitchen," I murmur as I run my hand along the island.

It takes a moment to locate some glasses, and my search yields some interesting information. While the kitchen looks ideal, very little of it gets used. Many of the dishes still have stickers on them, and most of the small appliances are in their boxes. It's like King has been building the perfect kitchen without any plans to actually use it.

I fill a glass with filtered water from the fridge, which is nearly empty, and peek a glance at the freezer, which is full to the brim of pre-packaged meals. That better fits my vision of King's adult life, though it doesn't explain the well-prepped kitchen.

With more questions than I had a moment ago, I return to King's bedroom and set the glass of water on his bedside table. He's already snoring softly, clearly exhausted from his gastrically disastrous afternoon. "I guess I'll hang out here until you wake up," I say. And then I take in the room.

Like the kitchen, the master bedroom has been expertly furnished and decorated. It has a masculine feel to it, full of dark woods and navy blues, and it feels very much like King. The man version of him, anyway. He looks at home in this place, and I can't help but wonder what his life has been like since I left.

He never had big plans for himself, content to keep doing the things he's been doing his whole life, and some of that still seems to be true. He's still at the surf shop. He still lives in Willow Cove, where he's lived his whole life. But he has clearly grown up and matured into adulthood. What else do I really know about him? Not much.

And yet I proposed to the man. Someone I can't say that I know anymore. Crazier still, he *agreed*.

I'm pretty sure this is a bad idea, but it's the only idea I've got.

Chapter Five

Georgie

I'M ELBOW-DEEP IN BISCUIT dough when King emerges wearing nothing but a pair of gym shorts and a confused expression. He takes in the messy kitchen, eyebrows pulling low, and then leans his shoulder against the wall at the edge of the kitchen. "Please," he growls, "make yourself at home."

I huff, hating the way my body tenses up at his rough tone. I shouldn't be afraid of this man, but he's as much a stranger as he was when we met at twelve years old. And he's a stranger who doesn't like me. I don't like being disliked any more than I like people telling me what to do. "Well, I would have asked for permission, but you were passed out."

I'm doing my best not to stare at him, but it's incredibly difficult. I saw him shirtless at the bakery, but only for a second or two. Now he's all on display, shoulders and abs dotted with droplets of water. He must have showered before coming to find me, and seeing him wet like this has memories of King on the ocean surfacing in my mind.

That was always my favorite time to see him, right after he'd been out on the waves. He always looked so happy and worry-free, and his hair tends to take on a mind of its own when it gets wet. It's not curly, not like mine, but it has a fun wave to it that fits his personality so well.

I clear my throat and start cutting biscuits with a glass cup. I already have a tray in the oven, and this is way more than the two of us could ever eat, but I bake when I'm stressed. In the kitchen, I can control the outcome instead of bracing myself for what might happen. Ever since Lane's unexpected breakup speech, I can't stop feeling like something bad is right behind me.

"How are you feeling?" I ask, trying to distract myself.

He moves closer, something I feel as much as I see out of the corner of my eye. The man has a *presence*. "Better. What are you making?"

"Can you call yourself a Southern boy if you don't recognize biscuits and gravy?" I look up and jump when I realize he's just on the other side of the island from me. It was hard enough not to stare at him when he was on the other side of the room. "I, uh, thought it might be nice to have some comfort food, if you're up to it."

In response, his stomach growls loudly and seems to break some of the tension between us. He relaxes, arms falling to his sides and giving me an up close view of his broad chest. "Thank you," he says slowly. "I don't know if I would have made it home on my own."

"Food poisoning?"

"Probably."

"What did you eat?"

We both glance at the garbage can, which is full of frozen meal packages.

He runs a hand through his hair, giving it some more life as the damp locks fall back into place. "Sorry about, uh..." He glances down at his bare torso. "I put in a load of laundry, but until it's done..."

"I'm not complaining." My words register as soon as they're out of my mouth, and I blush. Hard. "I didn't mean that how it sounded."

"It sounded like you were admiring me." There's only a hint of humor in his tone, which is less than I would have expected from him. He was always so carefree when we were young, and though I've seen pieces of the old King popping up here and there, he's so different from how I remember him. It's like life has weighed him down. "So..."

The first batch of biscuits is probably ready to come out of the oven, but my eyes lock on his forearms as he rests his hands on the counter. Surfing doesn't take a lot of forearm work, so I have to wonder where all this muscle is coming from. "So?" I repeat and then force myself to focus on the food. I don't want to serve King burned biscuits just because he's well-formed.

Thankfully, the biscuits are perfectly golden as I pull them out of the oven. I'm pretty sure I still need to convince him that getting married is a great idea, and plying him with food is always a good way to go.

Marriage really is the best way for us both to win. He gets someone to revive his uncle's legacy and help him keep Bill's memory alive, and I get my own place to make it how I want. Without the weird legal issue of the bakery having to stay with family, it would be such a simple trade.

When King says nothing, I grit my teeth and take a slow breath to work up the courage to ask him if he was serious when he agreed to my proposal. "Were you—"

"I don't like the idea of marrying you," he says. Nice and blunt.

I wilt. "Oh." Not wanting to look at him, I put a couple of hot biscuits on a plate with a side of sausage gravy from the pot on the stove, in case he's able to handle more than the biscuits on their own. "I just thought—"

"But you're right, and I need help." His dark eyes follow the plate as I set it in front of him.

"I can't actually buy it," I admit. It'll be better if I'm honest about that part up front. "I made pretty good money working on *Home Baked*, but New York is expensive."

"That's unfortunate." When I hand him a fork, he looks at it for a second and then takes it, though the jury is still out on whether he's going to eat my offering. "You did *choose* New York," he reminds me and then cuts off a piece of biscuit, dipping it in the gravy before he takes a bite. His face is suddenly a mixture of pleasure and frustration, like he's annoyed by how good it tastes. He swallows, looks down at the food as if trying to decide if he wants to talk or eat, and then he meets my gaze again. "Uncle Bill would have wanted you to have Kingston's. We both know that. You don't have to buy it, as long as you promise not to change anything."

I can't hold back the laugh that bubbles out of me. "Are you serious? No way."

He nods as he takes another large bite. "That's non-negotiable."

"Then you can kiss that bakery goodbye because it's never going to survive with the way it is now."

"All it needs is someone who can actually bake. I'm assuming that's you."

Your version of baking is different from mine, and it's just not what the company needs. I shove Lane's words aside, no matter how much they still sting two weeks later. "Assuming," I repeat, gesturing to King's quickly disappearing biscuits. "I'll have you know I was an award-winning pastry chef up in New York."

He rolls his eyes. "Debatable."

"How is a literal award debatable?"

"If I recall, you took third place." He grabs a couple more biscuits, making his way around the island to load them up with gravy. Apparently his stomach is handling the food just fine. "That's what Uncle Bill told me, anyway."

Folding my arms, I wait until he settles himself on a stool across from me and resumes eating. "I still got an award," I grumble. It makes me feel like a petulant child. "Regardless, it's going to take more than my skills in a kitchen to get Kingston's back to profitable. The place is falling apart."

"It has character."

"It has wood rot and a finicky oven. It needs to be updated, King."

"Fine. You can fix anything that needs fixing." He scowls. "I suppose you'll want to slap your own name on the door?"

Honestly, I hadn't thought about it, but I have a feeling he will put up a fight if I say anything but no. "Kingston's is already a known name. Seems silly to start from scratch."

"There's a positive, at least."

"So are we doing this?" If we're not, I'd rather not waste any more time around this grumbly man than I need to. He can drive me back to my car, and I can try to find some new plan for my life. No biggie.

King clenches his jaw, studying me for a moment before he swears under his breath.

I grimace. "Do I want to ask?"

"Vanderman is the estate attorney."

"So?" I don't think I've ever met the guy, but his wife used to be a regular at the bakery. She probably still is, and I remember her being nosier than a bloodhound. I can't see that being a problem, though. It's not like we'll be keeping our marriage a secret.

King shifts in his seat, looking uncomfortable. "So... He was Uncle Bill's best friend. He might need some...convincing."

I don't like the sound of that. "What kind of convincing?"

"The kind where he thinks we're really married."

I laugh again. "That's what a marriage license is for, isn't it?" A strange sensation runs through me, like I just got a shot of carbonation injected into my bloodstream. Shuddering, I turn to the sink and start washing the flour from my hands as I imagine standing in front of a judge, King standing next to me.

I imagined something similar when we were young and first started dating, though it was a priest then and we were on the beach in the glow of a gorgeous sunset. Marrying Royal Kingston had been a teenage fantasy, but that was before I realized there was a whole world out there.

Before I worried I would get stuck in Willow Cove and have nowhere to go but in circles.

King waits until I turn the water off before he speaks again. "Vanderman told me about the family stipulation about a month and a half ago, when I, uh, tried to sell the bakery to someone from Charleston."

I gasp. "You tried to *sell it*?"

He shrugs, eyes on his empty plate. "I was overwhelmed. And in mourning. Uncle Bill had only been gone for a week, and I wasn't thinking straight."

I can't imagine what some bigwig would have done with the place if King hadn't been stopped, and I shudder at the idea of Kingston's becoming a cookie cutter copy of every franchised multimillion-dollar company out there.

"Anyway," he says, "Vanderman was clear about the will's directive, and he also made it clear that he will uphold Uncle Bill's wishes. He's going to stand firm on that whole 'family' thing."

I fold my arms. "Again, a marriage license will make us family. You can't get any clearer than that."

King's gaze jumps up. "Not for Vanderman. He'll need to think this thing is real."

"How is anyone supposed to believe a spur-of-the-moment marriage to a stranger is real?"

Wincing, he shakes his head. "You're not technically a stranger, Georgie. Even if you feel like one."

Ouch. But at least I'm not the only one who feels like she doesn't know the person across from her. "What are you saying, King?"

"I'm saying we're going to have to make everyone in Willow Cove think you and I are in love if you're actually going to get the bakery."

My stomach flip-flops, and I have to grip the edge of the counter to hold myself steady. I was prepared to call King my husband, but this feels like more. This feels like my hold over my life is slipping even more than it already has. "Why don't we just hire a different attorney?"

King huffs a laugh and runs his hands down his face. "Georgie. Did you forget the part where I said Vanderman was Uncle Bill's best friend? Bill didn't trust anyone else, so how can I?"

I get that. But if we're stuck with a guy who will have to be convinced? "On paper only," I mutter, forcing myself to take slow, even breaths. "That's all I'm agreeing to."

"Then it's not going to work."

I groan. "You're telling me you're totally fine with pretending you don't hate me?"

"I don't ha..." He stops himself before he finishes the sentence, which doesn't feel great. He would be justified in keeping me low on his list of favorite people; I did turn down his proposal and leave him on an uninhabited island. "It would only be when we're in public together, which doesn't have to happen often. We'll both be too busy with our respective jobs to spend much time together."

"A bright spot of this plan," I say as I start cleaning up the mess I made with the biscuits. I'm still not sure why King's kitchen is so well-equipped, but getting it back to the spotless state it was in before will be a great distraction as this conversation continues. "And how is never spending time together going to convince Vanderman?"

"Ah. Right. Maybe... One date a week?"

"How about no dates? We can just visit each other at our respective places of business."

His expression hardens when I glance up at him. "You're not going to break my shelves again, are you?"

"Only if you throw up inside my bakery again."

"*It's not your bakery.*" The words come out sharp enough that I jump, and King cringes. "Sorry. I'm... Sometimes it doesn't feel real that he's gone."

Something inside me aches to pull him into my arms and comfort him, but this conversation does not feel like a good time to be friendly. It feels weird, talking about what our marriage is going to look like, because it's so different from how our talks used to sound. Granted, eighteen-year-olds don't have a great grasp on what adulthood will look like, but we used to sit on the beach and talk about how great it would be to work on the boardwalk together, drive home after a long day, settle on the couch and watch our favorite show...

It all sounded so magical back then. But that isn't how life works, and when I graduated and started thinking about what I wanted in life—about the dreams that could never be achieved here—I realized we were too naive. Too young to get married.

I probably should have told King as much instead of running away, but I'd known, even then, that he would have had an argument ready for me. *We can have a long engagement. We don't have to get married right away.* He never would have understood why I couldn't say yes.

He's never going to leave Willow Cove. I know that now as much as I knew it then. I loved him too much to risk resenting him when my dreams slipped away from me. Or him resenting me for not being content with a small but good life and wanting more. So I left.

"I don't know if we can do this," King says, probably reading my mind. If only he could have done that back then. Maybe he would have seen my fears and known not to push things too fast. Or at all.

I take a steeling breath. "I can do this. It's only temporary."

"Your favorite."

"What is that supposed to mean?"

"It means I only have to deal with you for a few months, which is probably the only reason I'll make it through in one piece."

I sneer a little, feeling my competitive nature rising. "I'm sorry this is going to be so difficult for you. You always did struggle with hard things."

"Okay." He stands, the stool scraping along the floor behind him, and folds his arms again. I'm pretty sure he's flexing, and it's taking everything in me not to look down and admire his well-toned torso. "I can handle this marriage, Georgie. I'm more worried about you running off before all is said and done and wasting my time."

His counter-attack stings, but he has a point. "I'm not going to run. Not until the bakery is thriving, anyway."

"And then what?"

I shrug, though I know he won't like me not having a solid plan beyond the immediate. "Then I figure out what to do from there. Maybe I'll find someone who can manage the place well enough so I can move on and use the profits to build my own thing. No matter what, I'll keep the place, so you don't have to worry about it disappearing."

He clenches his jaw but seems to accept that answer, nodding a little as he settles back on the stool. "So I'll stop by in the mornings," he says, returning to the original topic.

I sigh and start returning dishes to the cupboards so I don't have to look at him during this part. "I can bring you baked goods in the afternoons."

"If anyone asks, and they will, we recently reconnected."

"Which is true."

"Unfortunately."

I roll my eyes. "Are you going to be this grumpy all the time? Since when did you become a crotchety old man?"

"Since my girlfriend ran away without any word of explanation and disappeared." His gaze is cold when I look at him, but I can see the pain behind the ice. "Since she came back after *ten years* and pretended we didn't need to talk about it."

"Do you want to talk about it?"

"No."

I shouldn't be relieved, but I am. I know it's something we *should* talk about, but I am too good at avoiding confrontation to have any idea how that conversation might go. I'm not sure I would know what to say in the first place. Sometimes, when I look back at that day, I think I understand why I left the way I did, and other times I wish I could go back to that moment and really take my time understanding why the only emotion inside me when he dropped to one knee was terror.

Back then, it felt so much easier to think he would understand. He knew I wanted to start my own bakery someday, and I knew he wanted to stay close to his uncle, and I figured he would connect the dots and agree that it wasn't a good idea to get married.

Looking at him now, I don't think he connected anything. And I don't think Bill ever told King any of the stuff I told him over the years.

"King."

"No," he repeats. "Not now."

I check on the second round of biscuits in the oven and am grateful for the distraction as I take them out and turn the oven off. I know getting married is the simplest way we can both have the lives we want, but clearly it isn't going to be easy, no matter what either of us have said. And there's one important thing we haven't talked about when it comes to this union.

"Where am I going to live?" I ask as calmly as I can.

King grunts. "Wherever you want."

"If we're married…"

Clenching his jaw, he glances around his house as if it might have a solution that isn't the two of us living together. "Right. Logically, you would live here with me."

"I can take a guest room."

"No, you can't."

"It's not like anyone is going to be coming over to see where I sleep."

"Maybe not, but…" He rubs the back of his neck, looking a little sheepish. "I don't have a guest room."

I frown. "Then what are those two other rooms down the hall?" I noticed them when I went searching for the bathroom, which was the first door I came across, and it took all of my self-discipline to not go snooping through King's house while he was passed out on the bed. Maybe I *should* have snooped.

He coughs, folding his arms. "At the moment? They're construction zones. I've been remodeling, but they haven't been a priority lately."

Well that complicates things. I am for sure not sharing a bed with King, married or not. We can be adults about things, but I can't let proximity muddy the waters of this sham marriage. As a chronic sleep-walker with a lifelong tendency to cuddle anything nearby, I am not about to put myself anywhere near the man who hates me. He'd likely push me off the bed if I got too close.

"I guess I can sleep on the couch…" I say it with a casualness I don't feel. Maybe when I was twenty I could have done it, but over the last couple of years I've gotten used to sleeping on a mattress that cost more than three months' rent.

King barks out a short laugh. "Have fun with that, though I don't recommend it."

"Well, then what do you suggest? Share your bed?"

As the color drains from his face, he brings his plate to the sink and looks out into the wild backyard. "I have a pool house. It's been a couple of years since I last went in there, but..."

Oh. An actual solution. That's good. "Does this pool house have a bed?"

King looks back at me, and I really don't like the look of mischief in his eyes. Something tells me he's not going to make any of this easy on me.

Chapter Six

King

GRABBING A COUPLE MORE biscuits, I lead Georgie out the backyard and hope nothing has taken up residence in the pool house. When I first bought this place a few years ago, the pool house had been inhabited by a family of raccoons who were none too pleased to be evicted. I guessed the old owners, a retired couple who only came to the house every so often, didn't bother with the structure at the back of the property and had no idea they had furry little squatters.

Originally, I planned to rent out the pool house, since I have great access to a calm beach across the street that would be a draw to tourists, but so many other things kept me busy. Updating the surf shop, training other instructors during the off season, renovating first the kitchen and master and then the other bedrooms, helping Uncle Bill when he started getting sick...

Prince Harry lumbers over to the gate of his pen as soon as he sees me, his dark eyes examining Georgie behind me with a bit too much interest in the dimming light of dusk. She hasn't noticed the llama yet, too busy taking in the rest of the yard, and I'm not about to say anything. Instead, I hold out one of the biscuits to show him my offering and then duck just in time as the mad beast spits in appreciation of my gift.

Georgie screams when the wad of saliva splatters her in the face.

I snort. "Sorry, I should have warned you that he's...broken." Normally, llamas spit when they're agitated or angry as a sort of defense mechanism, but not Prince Harry. This guy thinks it's a way to show affection.

Now that he's unloaded his slimy gift, I hold the biscuit closer and smile when he grabs it excitedly. "Good boy."

Georgie scrubs her face with her sleeve, shuddering and looking like she's on the verge of running away as she stares at the five and a half feet of llama a few feet away from her. "Why do you have a giant goat?"

Patting Prince Harry's strong neck, I take a bite of the other biscuit and wish I grabbed more because I'm still starving. I'm loath to mention it to her, but she's gotten way better than when she was a teen. Maybe it's just that anything is better than a freezer meal. "Prince Harry is clearly a llama," I say through a mouthful of buttery goodness. "And he was Uncle Bill's."

"Oh." Georgie relaxes a bit. "I forgot how much he liked collecting animals."

I've found homes for most of my uncle's menagerie, but Prince Harry is a tough one, given he is huge, borderline suicidal, and unconventional in every way. But I think a part of me hasn't been able to part with the last of the animals Bill collected, just like it is going to be nearly impossible to fully let go of the bakery.

Georgie may have agreed to limit her changes, but I know her. She'll stick to her promise for a little while, and then her stubborn nature will kick in and she'll forget everything I've said to her about preserving Bill's legacy.

"So," she says, taking a step back from Prince Harry as he leans over the fence to smell her. "The pool house?"

Right. Just beyond Prince Harry's pen, the pool house looks like it's in decent shape, which is good. I have to hope the interior boasts the same because there is no way in heaven and earth that I am sharing a bed with Georgie. I'd rather sleep on the couch despite the fact that it isn't designed for that. It's great for reclining, but I know from too much experience lately that a full night on the couch is rough.

The door handle feels loose, but I open the pool house without any difficulties and breathe a sigh of relief when it all looks relatively untouched. It's a bit musty and dusty, but that's an easy fix.

"Ta da," I mutter.

Georgie pokes her head under my arm. "Um."

"It's this or the couch, unless you'd prefer to sleep on the floor." I would never let her do that—the guilt would eat me alive—but I would rather keep her options limited to anything that doesn't interrupt my already awful sleep.

Groaning a little, she ducks under me and steps deeper into the space. It's small—no need for a pool house to be much bigger than this—but it has a bathroom and a little kitchenette. More than enough to survive for a few weeks while we get everything settled and done.

"What about a bed?" she asks. Skepticism laces her words with a sharp edge. I nod toward the couch. "It's a sleeper sofa."

"Splendid." She grits her teeth as her eyes continue to take in the room. "Does the door have a lock?"

"Nope."

"What's to stop you from sneaking in here while I'm asleep?"

"Self-respect, mostly."

She throws a glare at me.

Chuckling, I fold my arms and lean against the door frame. "Georgie, this is Willow Cove. You'll be fine."

"I've never understood your misplaced trust in people."

I sigh. It's not that I trust everyone, but I like to see the good in people. Still... "You're right," I say slowly. "I should have learned better after I trusted you all those years ago."

I'm being unfair, and I know it, but Georgie's unexpected arrival this morning feels like opening old wounds, and I'm too tired to mask the hurt. I'll be better tomorrow. Hopefully.

"Well," I say, knocking on the door frame. "Goodnight."

"Wait, can you give me a ride back to my car? All my stuff is there."

I probably should, given she drove me here, but my stomach is still trying to eat itself and I haven't had a proper chance to be annoyed that she's back. So I shake my head. "But Marlin has a taxi service. I'm sure you can look up the number."

It takes a second for recognition to set in. "Wait, Marlin Abernathy? Like, the guy who talks to chickens and thinks he can understand them? Does he even have a driver's license?"

I shrug. "Good question. You should ask him." And then I head back to the house in case I crack and tell her I'll give her a ride. It would be the right thing to do, but I can't bring myself to be gallant tonight. Instead, I eat three more biscuits loaded with gravy and finish doing my much-needed laundry before heading to bed, wondering the whole time whether Georgie will come back or if she's opted to run away again.

I can't decide which outcome I want more.

"Rise and shine!"

Georgie jolts awake at my call, tossing blankets and pillows and nearly tumbling off the lumpy sleeper sofa. I shouldn't take this much pleasure from her disorientation, but I was pleasantly surprised to find her in the pool house this morning, which has put me in a strangely good mood. That, plus a clean pair of shorts and a decent night's sleep for once, has made today feel like a turning point in the right direction.

"Royal?" Georgie mumbles as she tries to untangle herself from the sheets. She's clearly still half asleep if she's back to using my real name. "What time is it?"

I glance out the open door behind me, where the sky is starting to warm from black to blue. "Time for you to get yourself over to the bakery, obviously. I'm assuming you got your car back?"

The pool house is practically overflowing with clothes. I don't remember her being a disorganized person, but then again I never went to the house her parents rented every summer. She always just appeared on the boardwalk. Maybe this is true Georgie and I dodged a messy bullet.

Groaning, Georgie slowly sits up and runs a hand over her wild curls. "It's not my bakery yet," she complains. "I didn't get to bed until after one."

"Not my fault." It's sort of my fault. If she really used Marlin to get back to the boardwalk, it likely took a lot longer than she planned for. He likes his detours. And then she would have had to bring all her stuff in from her car, and judging by the sheer volume of it all, it probably took a while.

I fold my arms, trying not to acknowledge my growing guilt for not helping her last night. I was sound asleep by nine and slept like a rock all night. "As for the bakery, I plan to spend my morning getting an appointment set up at the courthouse for later today, so I can't be there."

That wakes her up. "You want to get married *today*?"

"The sooner we tie the knot, the sooner I can file for a divorce." I shrug, though the words taste bitter in my mouth. I've always thought of marriage as a one-time thing, not something to take lightly. Uncle Bill never married, but he talked all the time about how it was a special agreement that I should treat with respect.

So much for that.

"Your mama raised you to treat women right," he used to tell me, "and I won't let you forget it."

He'd always liked my mom, from the day she met my dad, and Uncle Bill had been a staple in my life from the beginning. Dad was younger than Bill by several years, but they looked out for each other after my grandparents died, long before I was born. Bill was as much a parent to me as my real parents, rest their souls.

Kingstons have a habit of dying young, something I try not to think about. Dad was thirty when the car accident took him. Mom didn't reach forty before she got sick. Bill made it to fifty-five, so maybe I've got a decent chance if the pattern continues.

Probably not if I keep eating questionable food from the freezer aisle.

Georgie finally rolls herself off the bed, pulling my focus back to her, and tugs her phone free of the charging cord it's attached to. Then she swears. That's new. "It's dead. But I had it plugged in all night!"

"Ah, yeah, I should have mentioned that the outlets only work if the lights are on."

"Of course." Her eyes flick back to me, her gaze cold. She looks younger this morning than she did yesterday, probably because her hair is a mess and she's not wearing any makeup. She looks more like the girl I knew before, the one who couldn't care less about eyeshadow and contouring and hadn't yet figured out how to tame her curls. There was always a wildness about her. A sense of adventure and ambition.

I liked that Georgie.

"Are you going to bake some bread, or what?" I ask and force myself to look away. I don't need reminders of the girl I knew. Just the sight of her disheveled and undone is twisting up my insides. "I'll warn you, Meg doesn't like being left on her own, and you can't afford for her to quit on you."

And then I leave, heading straight for my truck so I can put some distance between us. I really shouldn't force Georgie to jump right into the morning baking, but it's not like I'm all that good at it anyway. Her work ethic will have her joining Meg in half an hour or less, and I meant it when I told her I planned to get us in front of Judge Delgado as soon as possible.

If I don't, I'm going to chicken out.

It's too early to call the courthouse, so I drive to the boardwalk. Coop won't be happy about my early visit, but this feels like the kind of situation a best friend should know about. Sure enough, he's still sound asleep in his boat house and looks like he doesn't have a care in the world. That's not true, but Coop would never admit he's got his own worries. Still, I need his easygoing nature this morning if I'm going to survive the day.

Grabbing a pillow, I smack him in the face at the same time I say, "Up and at 'em, Heyes!"

He wakes with a shout, almost as entertaining as Georgie's reaction this morning as he flails about. "Whosere?" When his eyes find me in the dimness of the cabin where he sleeps, he groans and falls back onto his pillow. "Someone had better be dying, Kingston."

I didn't used to be a morning person, but running the bakery necessitated that I change my habits. Coop, who flies tourists around in a floatplane, has no such reasons, and he's never been good with early wakeups.

"This is equally important as death," I tell him and lean against the driftwood table we built a while back. "I'm getting married today and need a witness."

He lifts himself onto one elbow, squinting at me as he yawns. "Yeah, definitely heard you wrong just now. I thought you said you're getting married."

I lift an eyebrow.

Taking a slow breath, Coop looks around the boat and then sits up. "Okay. Well, who's the lucky woman?"

I expected more from him. Most likely, he's gearing up to laying his thoughts all out there. Especially once he hears who my prospective bride is, he'll have plenty to say.

I fold my arms, prepping myself for his reaction. "Georgie Carpenter."

He blinks. "Georgie Carpenter."

"Yep."

"As in the Georgie Carpenter who used to make you think holding hands and walking along the beach was fun. The same one who called me an idiot on multiple occasions and had you so whipped that even during the school year you would rather video chat with her than get out of the house and live your life."

Heat rises up my neck. Coop wasn't thrilled when Georgie and I started dating. I always wondered if it was because I spent most of my free time with her rather than hanging out with the guys, and it's looking like I may have been right. There aren't many of us left in Willow Cove, but Coop has generally been as single as I have with no indication that that will ever change. Though it's not like Georgie and I will be married in truth, she's still going to take up some of my limited free time.

I barely see Coop as it is.

He's not done, adding one last qualification to his list. "You're talking about the woman who disappeared without a trace after she literally left you stranded on an island when you proposed to her?"

"Technically *you* left me stranded on an island. But yes." I wait for him to have any sort of reaction that isn't blank confusion. "That's the one."

His eyebrows dip low. "Can I ask *why* you're marrying Georgie Carpenter today?"

I explain the situation as succinctly as I can, growing more tense with every nod he gives me. He's being way too calm about all of this. "So we're heading to the courthouse today to make it official," I finish.

Coop takes a breath, his expression still decidedly empty, and then he climbs out of bed and stands in front of me so he can put his hands on my shoulders. "King, I mean this with all the sincerity of our lifelong friendship: you're an idiot."

Don't I know it.

Chapter Seven

Georgie

IT'S BEEN A LONG time since I last imagined my hypothetical wedding day with King, but it certainly wasn't this—standing in the judge's office lined with pegboard walls and maroon carpet that has seen ten years too many. I'm not even in a dress, though I did put on some nice slacks and my favorite pair of heels. They still don't bring me up to King's height, which is wildly unfair. I stopped growing at sixteen, and it feels like he grew six more inches after I left Willow Cove.

For some reason, the suit he's wearing is really highlighting the fact that this man is so much more than the boy I left.

While the judge shuffles through some papers, a throat clears in the corner of the room, pulling my attention that way for the millionth time. Cooper Heyes has been glaring at me from the moment I showed up at the courthouse like it's his personal mission to silently drive me out of town. He and I were never friends, but clearly he's holding as much of a grudge as King is.

Maybe that's because I sort of blackmailed Coop into flying me back to Willow Cove the night King proposed. And by sort of I mean absolutely. I needed a way off that island, and I couldn't have King sitting next to me during the flight back.

King brought his pilot friend here as a witness, and I have no idea if Coop thinks this marriage is legit or not. Regardless, he doesn't like it, and I still feel his glare even when I face forward again.

"Here we are." Judge Delgado finds whatever he was looking for and slides a paper and pen toward me. "If you'll sign here, Miss Carpenter."

That's it? I just write my name and then I'll be married? I know it's not real, but that marriage license looks very real, and no one but King—and Coop—knows I'm doing this. Not even my parents know, which will hopefully remain the case until after the divorce is final. Or indefinitely. I should have at least told Cecily so I would have someone on my side, though my best friend likely would have taken the first flight out of JFK and tried to stop me. All I've given her are a few vague texts so she knows I'm still alive, and she is not going to be happy with me when I fill her in later today.

"You can still change your mind," King mutters beside me. He smells far better than he did yesterday. Looks better too. Where I tossed and turned all night, King looks like he had the best sleep of his life.

I probably look like a mess, but it's not like King has noticed. He's barely looked at me once since showing up at the bakery around ten this morning and telling Meg that she'll need to handle everything herself for a couple of hours.

I swallow, surprised by the emotion that sits heavy in my throat. I'm *getting married*, and my husband-to-be can't stand me. This might be the stupidest decision I've ever made, but I don't have a lot of options. King doesn't either. We can make this work. *I* can make this work.

I scribble my name and hand the pen to King, who signs without hesitation.

"Are there any objections?" the judge asks, looking at Coop.

He rolls his eyes. "Yeah, but that's not going to stop them."

"Very well." Given the nature of this marriage, we probably should have brought in some lawyers, but it's too late now. The judge declares us husband and wife and invites us to kiss if we choose.

It seems weird not to, but my new husband would have to look at me for us to take that step. And it's probably weird if we *do* kiss. This isn't a real marriage, and we're going into it with the knowledge that it is going to end as soon as it can.

Still, I look at King and wonder what's going through his head. I doubt he would have even considered this arrangement if he wasn't desperate, but I'm not sure how I feel about him being completely unaffected by our sudden change in marital status. He claimed to love me at one point—he said it many times, in fact—and I still have occasional moments when I wonder what might have been if I had stayed.

"Mr. Kingston?" The old judge leans forward, glancing between us because neither of us have moved. "Are you alright, son?"

King blinks, his eyes slide over to me, and then suddenly his mouth is on mine. A hundred memories come rushing back with the feel of his lips, but he's gone before I can react or respond, pulling away and taking my hand.

"We need to get back to work," he says and tugs me to the door. "Thanks, Judge Delgado."

"Anytime," the judge replies. "Well, not anytime, obviously. You only get married once."

Suddenly I feel slightly sick. Maybe I caught the bug King had yesterday. I think I may have crossed too far into the "anything to get the job done" side of my personality, but it's too late to go back now.

Coop silently follows us out, hands in his pockets and enough judgment in his expression to say everything he's holding back.

None of us say anything until we reach King's truck. I'm still feeling a little off balance from that kiss, so I just stand here and try to process the notion that I'm a married woman now. A *wife*. That's my husband standing next to me with his jaw clenched and a whole lot of something brewing behind his eyes.

"Coop," he says eventually, "you'll help make sure everyone thinks it's real?"

I frown, glancing between the two men. "You told him it's fake?"

King shrugs. "Why wouldn't I?"

"Because he could tell other people."

"He wouldn't do that. Would you, Coop?"

Coop lifts an eyebrow but says nothing, which is not at all reassuring.

Folding my arms, I do my best to look fierce, though it's hard to feel like I have any leverage when I'm boxed in by two large men. I am not starting off this marriage, no matter how short it will be, by being pushed around. "You do realize that we're married now, which means we're in this together, right? You can't make decisions about this arrangement without my input."

King matches my stance, and of course he looks way more impressive with his large arms and broad shoulders. "You're telling me you haven't given Cece all the details of this *arrangement*?"

"How do you know about Cece?"

He lifts one shoulder. "Well?"

"No, I haven't told her...yet." I tack that last word on reluctantly. "But it's not the same when she isn't in Willow Cove. Coop is here, and he knows all the people we have to convince that we are happily married."

"You're doing a terrible job of it, by the way," Coop mutters, frowning at each of us in turn. "Do I need to be worried about the two of you strangling each other in the middle of the night? And I don't mean that as a euphemism."

I groan. "Why are you still here?"

Shrugging, he starts looking at the sky with disinterest. "Because King is my ride back to Coral Berry. If you want my opinion..."

"I don't," I grumble.

"You should show up at the boardwalk together. Half the town probably knows what just went down in the courthouse."

"Already?" It was so much easier to keep things a secret in New York, where people minded their own business. "Ugh, I *hate* small towns."

Maybe I imagine it, but King winces a little before he digs his keys out of his pocket and hands them to Coop. "We're planning a honeymoon at the end of the season, when everything calms down and we don't have businesses that need our attention." He says it in a way that is clear he's expecting his friend to help spread that explanation for why we're going back to our day like nothing has happened instead of celebrating our nuptials.

Coop nods. "Fine. Just remember I've got an extra cot in the boat house if you need an escape." He gives King a pointed look, throws another glare toward me, and then climbs into King's truck and drives off.

And now I feel entirely awkward, which is exactly how a girl wants to feel on her wedding day with her new husband. "So."

King narrows his eyes. "So."

"You kissed me."

"I had to make it look real."

"Are you going to have to do that a lot?"

"Hopefully not."

"Agreed." Honestly, I'm not sure if I say that because I don't want him to kiss me or because I *do*. I did plenty of dating over the last ten years and got my fair share of kisses, but something about King's kiss is still buzzing around inside of me. I don't like it. "We should probably lay down some more specific rules when it comes to being out in pub—"

"Is that Royal Kingston I see?" An older woman sashays across the parking lot with the grace of a waddling goose, her gray hair making a valiant effort to escape the braid it's in. She has a wide smile on her face, but the look in her eyes is anything but friendly. "I just heard the craziest thing about you."

Before I can even try to remember if I know this woman, King tugs me up against his side and splays his hand at my waist. Goodness, did his hands get bigger too? Heat spreads through me from his fingers to the tip of my nose, and it was already hot outside to begin with. I'm probably beet red right now.

"Mrs. Pinnock," he says cheerfully. "I'd bet you're glad to have school over for a few months. What adventures have you and Carl planned for this summer?"

She clucks her tongue at him. "Now now, Royal, you won't distract me that easily." Her eyes stray over to me, sliding from my head to my toes and making me burn even warmer. "Who is this delightful little miss?"

She's clearly asking the question of King, even though her eyes are still fixed on me. It's like she's expecting me to stand here in silence, which has never been my style.

I hold out a hand. "Georgie Carp—" I yelp when King's fingers dig into my side. It's as much the tickle of it as it is the proximity I haven't had a chance to process. "Georgie," I repeat, leaving off my last name. I have no plans to change it, but I can see why it will confuse people if I go around advertising myself as *not* a Kingston.

"My wife," King adds. His voice isn't as strong as it was a second ago. The words seem to fall out of him, and his grip on my waist tightens, making me squirm again.

Mrs. Pinnock's mouth falls open in a large O as she ignores my outstretched hand entirely. "Your...your wife? Surely not."

"Surely yes," I argue, forcing what I hope is a loving smile as I lean into King and look up at him. "At least, I'm hoping it was a marriage license we just signed and not a contract with the devil."

"I'd never share you with the devil," King says. More like *growls*. He moves me so I'm directly in front of him now, both arms tucked around me, and then presses a kiss to my neck.

My whole body erupts in goosebumps, and I have to put all my focus into breathing. The old King never pulled *that* move.

"But..." Mrs. Pinnock looks like she wants to both argue against our marriage and call us out for being indecent in public. She waits another moment, during which King leaves a trail of kisses up to my ear, and then she waddles toward the courthouse without another word.

As soon as she's out of sight, King takes a step away from me and leaves a chilled gap between us. "That was the high school principal, by the way," he says calmly. "I told you about her before, right? She'll verify that we really did get married, and then she'll spread the word that the rumors are true." How does he look so normal right now? I feel like I might melt into the pavement. "We should really get back. I have to open the surf shack, and Meg doesn't like being on her own for long."

Swallowing a huge gulp of air, I hold it in my lungs until my heart stops trying to beat out of my chest. Then I lead the way to my car, telling myself that I'm being ridiculous. There's no reason for me to have that kind of reaction to the man when he's only going to be in my life for a few weeks. No matter how attractive he is, he's never going to be more than a means to an end.

I made sure of that when I ran away.

We're halfway to the boardwalk when I finally speak. "Maybe don't do that again." I figure being direct is the only way I'll protect myself from more unexpected contact with the man next to me.

King keeps his eyes out his window. "Yep. Other rules?"

"Hand-holding is fine," I decide out loud. "But I'd like a warning if you ever think a kiss is necessary."

"Likewise. And if you could avoid smiling at me, that would make this a lot easier."

I scoff. "I can't smile at you? Why not?"

His jaw clenches so tightly that a muscle bulges near his ear.

Though I wish I could get a better look at his face, I force my eyes back to the road as I drive. "Are you *attracted* to me, Royal?"

He groans. "There was a time when I wanted to marry you, Georgie. Of course I'm attracted to you. And don't call me that."

"I don't think you ever told me why you don't like your name."

"Because it's ridiculous."

I finally feel like I'm relaxing, and I need to embrace this feeling as long as I can. As soon as we get to Coral Berry Boardwalk, we'll have to perform again. "I always liked the name Royal."

"You're not the one who had to grow up with the name *Royal Kingston*."

"No, but now everyone is going to think I'm Georgie Kingston, which isn't much better. They might as well call me King George."

He finally turns his head and gives me a glance, some of the tension leaving his body. "Yeah, that's pretty bad. Maybe I should take your name."

"And be named Royal Carpenter?"

He snorts. "Definitely not."

We settle into a sort of silence until I pull into the parking lot off the boardwalk. The ocean is rolling in the distance, wispy clouds floating lazily above the horizon, and a soft breeze brushes across the grasses in the sand. Willow Cove really is beautiful, and I missed the beaches and the sunshine. Yeah, New York has sun too, but it's blocked out by all the skyscrapers and pollution.

I can breathe here in a way I couldn't there.

"Well..." King says, unclipping his seatbelt and sitting up straight. "Back to work?"

I grimace. "We're going to have to tell Meg that we just got married," I say, wishing I'd spent more than a few hours with the young woman. She seems to like me well enough, but this is kind of a big thing. "Something tells me she's not going to like that."

All of the tension floods back into King's body, and I almost grab his hand to offer some sort of comfort. But I don't. "Oh, she's going to hate it," he says. "I didn't think about that."

"It will just take some time for her to get used to—"

"No." He shakes his head and then slips out of the car, waiting until I'm outside as well before he explains. "Meg is..." He squirms a little, his face twisting up as if he's searching for the right words. "She, uh... I..." Then he blushes.

I gasp. "Were you and Meg mixing business with pleasure?" I instantly hate the idea.

"No!" He runs a hand through his hair, which doesn't seem to be enough to ease his discomfort because he tugs his tie loose and slips out of his suit coat as well. He looks around, probably making sure no one is nearby, and then he lowers his voice. "No, of course we weren't. I would never... She seems to like me. I mean, she looks at me like..."

I fold my arms. "Like you're one of the most attractive men in Willow Cove? Well, obviously. Look at you."

My comment only deepens the color in his face, and he growls a little as he starts pacing. "Georgie, that's not helping."

"What? You said it about me."

"Exactly. I don't..." He stops with a huff, and for the first time since he found me on the boardwalk when I first got here, he seems to drop whatever walls he's put up so now I can really see him. He looks lost. Worn down. Even more so than before. "I don't know how to navigate this, Georgie. With our history, this is...complicated."

The relief at knowing I'm not the only one who is getting confused by all this falls flat when I realize what he's saying. "This marriage isn't real, King."

"I know that." But he frowns as he leans on the hood of my car, staring at the metal beneath his fingers. "And it has to stay that way. I can't get caught up in your orbit just for you to leave me drifting again."

His surprising admission shouldn't sting, but it does. I know I hurt him when I left, but it's not like I was the only one in that relationship. I wouldn't have ended things if he had just talked to me before dropping to one knee. Everything was changing at the end of that summer, and he decided he knew what was best for me.

"I'm not meant to be in a place like this forever," I whisper, speaking as much to the King of ten years ago as to the one in front of me.

He looks up, his dark eyes meeting mine in a way that makes him look the same way he did back then. This man is so *good*, and any woman would be lucky to be loved by him. But his life is here and always will be, and I've never been able to imagine myself staying in this town forever.

"How do we do this?" he asks quietly.

I shrug. "One day at a time?"

"Okay."

"Or maybe one moment at a time."

"Even better."

I grab a pair of tennis shoes from the back seat, since I'm not about to stand in a bakery for hours in my heels, and then I look at King with determination. "First things first, I'm going to make *you* tell Meg that I'm your wife."

He winces. "No, see, I thought it would go over better if *you* did that."

Yeah, definitely not taking on that task. "But she knows you better."

"You're less likely to get slapped."

I can't help but laugh. Meg seemed nice enough when I worked with her, and it sounds like King never really gave her any signs that he might be interested. Unless he did without realizing it, which seems more likely than he thinks. If he's anything like the guy I knew, he was probably plenty friendly and unknowingly filled her with hope.

I start walking toward the boardwalk, knowing King will follow because he always does. But now I have his orbit analogy in my head, and I can practically feel him behind me like he's the moon to my planet, tugged along with me while I take my own path. Was it always that way?

"I'm not going to say a word to her," I tell him, shaking away the unease that starts building in my belly. King is doing me a huge favor—monumental—by giving me his uncle's bakery, and I don't want him to feel like he's being steamrolled. Outside of this Meg problem, anyway. "So unless you want her to hear the news from one of the regulars, you're going to be the one to break it to her."

He swears under his breath and then picks up his pace to walk even with me. "I forgot how stubborn you can be."

"No, you didn't."

"No, I didn't. But I hoped you grew out of it."

I snicker. "I grew out of a lot of things, like skinny jeans and A cups, but I like to think I've only gotten more hard-headed."

I can almost feel his eyes stray to my chest, though he quickly forces his gaze forward again as he says, "Is that why your boyfriend dumped you?"

The question catches me so off guard that my foot catches on a slightly raised plank of wood, tripping me. The only reason I don't faceplant is because King grips my elbow.

"Sorry," he says as he helps me up. He doesn't sound all that apologetic. "I was curious if it was a creative differences sort of thing or if he got annoyed by your stubbornness too many times."

"How do you even know about that?" I had planned to never mention Lane, seeing as my past relationship has no bearing on this one outside of the breakup being the reason I ended up here.

"Your stubbornness? It's your defining feature." He chuckles when I glare at him. I don't think he's trying to be mean—I don't know if he's capable of being truly *cruel*—but I wouldn't be surprised if this is his way of putting up some walls between us again. I'll accept it, but only because those walls are going to be necessary if we want things to stay black and white.

"Coop," he says when I don't respond to his teasing. "Apparently he's a fan of your show."

"It's not my show. Not anymore." And as much as I never loved being on TV, Lane's unilateral decision to kick me out will never sit easy with me. I know things were rough between us, but I didn't think they were *that* bad. How many signs did I miss because I was so focused on what was ahead of me? It's ironic how much time I spent trying to make sure things were working so I could control what happened, only for that determination to be the reason I lost control entirely.

I fold my arms around myself and sigh. "We should really get to the bakery and tell Meg that we're married so she knows she works for me too now."

Thankfully, he accepts my deflection and nods. "Yeah, I've got a lesson in an hour, so I should get that slap sooner than later so it has some time to fade."

Meg doesn't slap King, which seems to genuinely surprise him, but she does glare daggers at him when he leaves the bakery. She doesn't seem to know what to do with me now that I'm not just a helping hand, eventually choosing to pretend I don't exist as she goes about her tasks, and I decide I should probably watch my back from here on out.

Just in case.

Chapter Eight

King

I'M ALWAYS SO MUCH happier on the water.

Taking my first student of the season out to try some waves feels like plugging in a piece of my soul that fell out two months ago when the last of my family slipped away. As I straddle the board, giving my student a few minutes to get comfortable on his own board, I tilt my head back and soak up the sun. I'm always eager for summer, when I have enough students to keep me busy and my shop really takes off, but things got a lot more complicated when Bill got sick.

I haven't had a peaceful moment like this in months, and now that I have a wife, I doubt I'll have many for a long time to come.

A wife. *Georgie.* It's been three hours, and it still doesn't feel real. And yet...

I can't get the name Georgie Kingston out of my head, which is going to be a problem even if she has no plans to actually change her name. It's like she was meant to be part of my family, which for generations has been of the opinion that only the names of the British monarchy are acceptable. Uncle

Bill—William—and my dad, Edward, were only a small part of the Henrys and Elizabeths and Charleses that have made up my pedigree pretty much since the first colonizers arrived in what is now the eastern United States.

Maybe that's why Kingstons don't live to see old age. It's our own hubris in thinking we deserve such lofty names.

I always liked the name Royal.

Georgie is the only person I ever willingly allowed to use my first name, and a part of me loves hearing it on her tongue again. I shouldn't let her, but after our little truce this morning on the way back from the courthouse, my resolve is slipping. Ten years ago, I would have died happy being able to say that Georgie is my wife. Now... Now, I have to make sure I don't let myself start to think any of it is real. She said herself that she's not going to last long once she gets the bakery in her name, and then she'll be gone.

Just like before.

I shake my head and return my focus to the man in front of me. "Okay, Sean, how are you feeling?"

He's shaking a little as he bobs in the water with me, but the ocean is pretty calm today. Maybe a little too calm to get any good surfing in, but it's perfect for his first time. "I'm feeling pretty good," he says, his voice bouncing with nervous excitement.

We spent half an hour practicing his take off on the beach, and he's been paddling around for a good fifteen minutes to get the hang of moving around on his board. If he's going to try surfing, now's as good a time as any.

"Ready to try to hit a wave?" I ask, almost hoping he says no so I can have an excuse to stay out here a little longer. The shop will be open for a few more hours, until the sun goes down, but I've got Brody behind the counter. I don't have any other lessons today, which means there's nothing holding me back from heading to the bakery and making sure Meg hasn't murdered Georgie with a cake knife. She wasn't happy when I left, and I don't think her anger was entirely directed at me.

I probably shouldn't have left Georgie there on her own.

"I'm ready!" Sean says with a lot more enthusiasm than I expect, given his hesitation so far. Then again, the guy did jump at the chance to move his lesson to today after I bailed on him yesterday, so he has probably been wanting to learn for a while.

I walk him through the process of getting out to the point where the waves are starting to break, telling him how to feel the waves and know when he needs to start paddling. "You're going to miss a lot of the waves," I warn him. "And even if you get up, you're bound to fall. A lot. Just make sure you fall away from the beach so you don't get hit with your board."

He's got a foam board, so it's less dangerous than my fiberglass, but I'd still prefer he avoid getting whacked in the head if he falls forward instead of back. When I started teaching lessons as a teen, one of my first students got knocked unconscious by his board, and I'd never been so terrified in my life. The guy was fine in the end, but I've been more cautious ever since.

We get in position and face the beach, looking behind us for the next good wave.

"This could be it," I tell Sean, grinning when he gets in the perfect position. "Okay, start paddling when I tell you, and as soon as you feel your momentum pick up with the wave, stand up. Ready? Go!"

He paddles wildly but doesn't get up in time to catch the wave. He seems okay about the mistake and simply gets back in position, a little more eagerness in his face.

It takes three more tries before he catches a good one and gets up on his feet, and he rides a few yards before tumbling sideways.

"That was awesome!" I tell him when I reach him. I help him back onto his board, and we get into position again. "Do you feel how you need to balance?"

"I think so."

After another forty minutes, we head back to shore, and Sean tells me he's going to recommend me to all his friends the next time they come to Willow Cove on vacation. I smile and thank him, chatting for a few more minutes as I stow his board and help him out of his wetsuit, but I know I'll never see him again. I rarely do. There have been a couple of people over the years who come

back, either for a refresher lesson or to say hi, but outside of the rich folk
who have permanent summer houses here, Willow Cove tends to be a one
and done destination.

I'm fine with that. Summers get crazy as it is, and the last time I inter-
acted with a regular visitor, I got my heart broken.

With Sean gone, I return to the shop and grab my phone from behind
the counter to check my messages, chuckling when I see several texts from
Coop asking if Georgie and I have killed each other yet. I'm not going to
bother gracing him with a response, especially because I watched him fly
off with some tourists not long ago so he'll be plenty busy for a while.

I know he's not happy about my decision to agree to Georgie's plan, but
I really hope he eventually remembers that it's more helpful for me to have
his support than blanket criticism. What's done is done.

"Hey, King," Brody says as he finishes straightening the wall of snorkel
masks for purchase, "I just heard from Lacey, and it sounds like she's coming back to Willow Cove after all. You're still wanting another instructor,
right?"

I grin as a bit of stress trickles away. "Yes! I would love to have her back
for the summer." I have two other instructors, including Brody, but I was
worried we wouldn't be able to handle everything on our own. Lacey had
other plans for her summer between semesters, leaving us one teacher short.
Last summer we could barely cover demand for surf lessons with the four
of us, and I'm expecting this year to be the same. Having Lacey on the team
will keep us from getting overwhelmed. "I'll send her a text," I tell Brody
and then look around the shop, searching for something to do.

Next week won't be this quiet, and I should take advantage of this free
time while I have it. I've set up an appointment with the estate attorney,
Mr. Vanderman, but it's not until three days from now. That's three days
we'll need to be convincing so he has no reason to think this marriage is a
sham.

His wife was in the bakery when Georgie first came into town, which
means she witnessed my cold greeting. That's not going to do us any favors.

"So what's with the suit?" Brody asks. He comes behind the counter with me, nodding toward the suit I left hanging in the back office. "Going to a funeral or something after work?"

I laugh. Kind of feels like it. "Actually..." Since he's going to find out eventually, I might as well throw it out there before he hears some convoluted version of my out-of-the-blue wedding. "I sort of got married this morning."

Brody blinks. Glances at the suit, then at my hand, and back to my face. "How do you sort of get married?"

"I did get married." I curl my fingers into fists and make a note to talk to Georgie about finding some rings. Apparently our bare hands are feeding everyone's doubt. "I know it feels like it came out of nowhere, but it didn't."

Frowning, Brody grabs a stool and settles himself down, like he's too confused to stand anymore. "But you weren't dating anyone. Were you?"

"Technically, no, but—"

"Was it some sort of bet? A dare? Does she need a green card?"

"Whoa." I hold my hands up, unable to stop the grin that spreads across my face even though my smile seems to confuse Brody just as much as the whole marriage idea. "It's nothing like that." Okay, so it's something like that, but he doesn't need to know that. "Georgie and I go way back, and we recently reconnected." That's a phrase I'm going to get tired of really fast.

At nineteen, Brody would have been too young to ever know Georgie in connection with me back then, but I do know he's been a longtime fan of Kingston's Bakery. In fact, Bill's the one who told me I should hire him when Brody turned sixteen because Brody had been hanging around the bakery for years in between surf runs.

Curious, I ask, "Do you remember about ten years ago a girl who worked at Kingston's during the summer? She had really curly brown hair and made the best cookies."

Brody thinks about my question for a moment, and then his eyes light up. "Oh yeah! I thought she was cute."

I frown. "She was like eight years older than you."

Shrugging, Brody grabs a rag and starts wiping down the counter. "Still thought she was hot."

"That's my wife you're talking about," I grumble.

Thankfully, he looks properly chagrined as he looks over at me and turns bright red. "Oh. But wait, that means she's back in town?"

My response is a mere growl.

"I just mean is she at the bakery again? I haven't had her cookies in so long."

Sighing, I nod. "Yeah, she's back at the bakery. She'll be running it now so I can spend more time here."

"Sweet! Think she'll give me free snickerdoodles if I tell her I work for you here?"

Grabbing another rag, I chuck it at him and then roll my eyes when he laughs. "I guess that's up to her," I grumble. "Are you good to close up? I want to go see my wife."

"Yeah, I can—wait! You said you got married this morning? Why aren't you on a honeymoon or something?"

This topic is going to get old as well. "Because we have too much work to do. We'll do something later."

"Okay, but why didn't you take today off so you could...you know." He waggles his eyebrows. "I could have taught that surf lesson, and no one came into the shop while you were out on the water. You could have been enjoying your first day as a married couple."

I force my mind not to go where Brody's comment implies. It takes some effort, especially after that kiss I shared with Georgie in the courthouse, which I still feel even hours later. For my own sanity, I really hope I don't have to get that close to her again, or I'm going to fall right back to where I was the last time she was here. Only, it'll be so much worse this time.

This time, we're not teenagers holding hands and stealing quick kisses. We're grown adults who are legally bound to each other. Georgie is a full-blown woman with curves and full lips and a stubbornness that shouldn't be as attractive as it is. That courthouse kiss, however short it was, reawakened a part of me that probably should have stayed dead.

"I'm going to the bakery," I mutter, ignoring Brody's suggestive whistle as I cross the sand to the stairs back up to the boardwalk.

Though I shouldn't be surprised, Kingston's is crowded when I step inside. Most of them look like locals, which means they're as much here for the gossip as they are for baked goods. Bracing myself, I keep to the back of the lobby and take it all in. Nothing is physically different, but the bakery already feels like it has changed. Something about the smell, the stocked displays, and the satisfied looks on the faces of those who have already been served.

It feels like Georgie.

Before I can stop them, memories of the first time I met Georgie start to surface.

I was twelve and already obsessed with surfing, so I was heading to the beach with a goal to spend the whole day on the water. But I had to make a stop at the bakery because my mom asked me to bring something to Uncle Bill, and I was reluctantly a good kid (and a little hopeful that I could steal some cookies in the process). The plan was to get in and out as quickly as possible, which resulted in me barreling into the lobby and colliding with a girl who had been about to dig into a strawberry cupcake as she walked out.

When I close my eyes, I can still see the way pink frosting spread across her nose and mouth as the cupcake smashed between us, and I swear I still have a bruise from our heads colliding. But once the proverbial dust settled after the crash, while we were still lying in a heap on the floor, my eyes fixed on hers, marveling at how green they were.

She smiled and said, "That's one way to eat a cupcake, I guess."

Then she licked the frosting from her lips, and it was the first time I thought about kissing someone even though I was nowhere near brave enough to do it. Thank goodness her parents stepped in, breaking us apart, and Uncle Bill offered them half a dozen cupcakes on the house to make up for my bumbling clumsiness.

By some miracle, Georgie said hi to me the next day when she and her parents visited the beach, and again when I was wandering the boardwalk with some friends. And by the end of the summer, she was spending as much time with me as she did with her family, and I begged for her email so we could keep in touch when she went back to New Hampshire.

Those emails were my lifeblood during the months of the year when Willow Cove's population dropped to nothing. From the beginning of September to the end of May, I hung on Georgie's every word and in turn told her everything, talking to her in a way I didn't talk to anyone else.

She was there for me when my mom died right before I turned fifteen, even if she was hundreds of miles away.

Every June for five years straight, I hung out around the bakery for days until she finally arrived and brought everything back into balance again. I knew I wanted to marry her when I was sixteen because there was no way anyone else could come close to matching her. She was it for me.

I even waited the summer after she left me, a part of me hoping she would come back again and finally give me an answer to my question. Her parents came, but she didn't, and I told myself to move on.

When Georgie comes gliding from the kitchen with a tray of vibrantly colored cupcakes, including some with pink frosting, my chest grows tight at the sight of her. *My wife.* The woman I clearly didn't move on from, which means I'm in a lot of danger right now.

"King!"

I don't know who shouts my name, but that one word pulls the entire lobby's attention to me where I'm standing by the door. Even Georgie and Meg, who is at the cash register, look over at me. Meg's expression is still furious, but there's confusion and something else in there too. It almost looks like worry. Georgie turns a bright red, which she tries to hide by darting back into the kitchen without acknowledging me.

That's going to make selling this marriage a little more difficult.

There's a part of me that has wanted this whole thing to fail from the beginning, but now that I'm standing in the last place that holds pieces of my family, I know deep in my bones that I'll never be able to give this a half-hearted effort. I need Georgie to keep this bakery alive, and Georgie needs her independence. I know better than to hold her back and stifle her free-spirited nature. Her stubbornness, for all its annoyance, is what has made her so good at what she does, and she can save this place.

She might be the only one who can.

Before I can take a step in any direction, half a dozen people crowd around me.

"Is it true that you and Georgie got married?" a man asks. "Marlin said she's staying at your house."

"Have you been secretly dating all this time?" a woman asks, pressing a hand to her heart. She's one of the teachers at the elementary school and clearly a romantic, with the way she looks like she's on the verge of a delighted swoon.

"What about her fancy boyfriend in New York?"

I frown at the woman who asks that question. I'm not sure I like the idea of everyone knowing about Georgie's fame thanks to that baking show and her stupid ex-boyfriend. She never did say why they broke up, but I know the guy was an idiot. According to Coop, he broke up with her on live TV only a couple of weeks ago.

Clenching my jaw, I debate the merits of answering any of their questions and then decide it would be easier to let them wonder. Until we can get the process of transferring the bakery underway, I don't want to confirm anything that could get us into trouble.

"Excuse me," I say and push forward, ducking around people until I get behind the counter and through the swinging kitchen door.

Georgie is waiting for me, a wild look in her eyes. She grabs my hands and shifts me a step to the left, and then she bites her lip as she glances behind me. "I'm going to kiss you, King," she says, and that's the only warning I get before her mouth is on mine.

Chapter Nine

Georgie

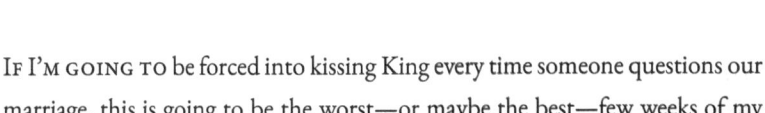

IF I'M GOING TO be forced into kissing King every time someone questions our marriage, this is going to be the worst—or maybe the best—few weeks of my life.

He's stiff at first, likely caught off guard by my sudden attack, but when I don't let him pull away—this one is going to need to be extra convincing—he relaxes enough to wrap his hands around my waist and gently tug me closer so we're not standing at an awkward distance. There's something intense about this kiss, in the way his lips move against mine with more pressure than the last time, but I am particularly grateful that he doesn't let it slip past PG.

I think I would enjoy that a little too much.

I'm the one who breaks the embrace, though King keeps me close to his body.

"Was that enough?" he asks, his eyes closed and a slightly pained expression on his face. If I had to hazard a guess, he liked that kiss as much as I did and hates himself for it.

Taking a steadying breath, I nod and then sigh. "Meg was being...difficult."

"How so?"

We're both whispering, just in case, but I don't anticipate Meg coming back here. She was hot on King's heels when he came back to the kitchen and would have seen that kiss, clear as day.

"She came to the conclusion that there's something fishy about our marriage and that it has something to do with the bakery."

King finally opens his eyes, his frown deep. "That's a pretty specific assertion," he mutters, dropping his hands from my waist and taking a step back. His eyes start wandering the bakery and the mess I've left behind.

I wouldn't normally be this disorganized, but I've been stress-baking ever since King left, cooking up way more than we could ever sell in a day. Then again, it feels like half the town has come into the store since I got back from the courthouse, determined to find out the truth for themselves. I've kept myself occupied back here to avoid their questions, and I'm sure Meg is irritated by being forced up front.

Yesterday, she was the one in charge and I was the helper. Today, she realized she now works for me instead of King and has been seething ever since. I can't say that I blame her for being a little salty.

"I don't know where she got the idea," I say, wiping my hands on my messy apron. "But I haven't had many good ways to convince her that she's wrong. I came to town *yesterday*, and now I'm married to you and taking over the bakery? I think anyone is going to come to the same conclusion if they think about it hard enough."

"Which is a problem, if we want this to work."

"Do you?" I ask the question without meaning to and wince when King's eyes meet mine. "I mean, you weren't exactly thrilled by this idea at the start, and you're not getting much out of the arrangement. It's hard to believe you *do* want this to work." I should probably stop talking now.

Leaning against the counter, King folds his arms and sighs. "I still don't like the idea," he admits. "But we both need the outcome. I can't keep running this place and, honestly, I can't trust it to anyone else."

I accept the praise with a small smile. I still plan to make some upgrades and changes as soon as I can, but I'm hoping I can do it in a way that will satisfy him. "Thank you. I know I don't deserve that trust."

"No, you don't." There's no bite to his words. He looks at the swinging door and sighs. "There are a lot of people out there who want answers."

"I know. I've been avoiding them all day."

"We should probably tell them something."

"What do you suggest?"

For an answer, he holds out his hand to me. I take it with some measure of hesitation, wishing I could read his mind as easily as he used to read mine. "Maybe we show them," he says and tugs me toward the lobby.

What in the world does that mean?

As we step through the door, the buzz of conversation in the lobby hushes and leaves the air thick with anticipation. King's dark eyes take everyone in before he puts a gentle hand on Meg's shoulder.

"I'll take over," he tells her. "I'm sure you're sick of being at the register."

Though relief washes across her face, it's short-lived. She glances between the two of us before returning her attention to King. "Are you sure your *wife* is okay with you giving orders?" She speaks the word "wife" with all the vitriol of a woman scorned. It's a bit dramatic for a woman as young as her, but I'll give her a pass today. We did spring our marriage on her. And everyone else.

I don't know why they think it's any of their business, but the crowd holds their breath as they wait for King's response to Meg's question.

He doesn't even look at me, keeping his eyes on her. His expression is patient and sympathetic, more like the man I remember and a far better sight than the tired and grumpy scowl I received yesterday. "That's still my name on the door, isn't it? And it wasn't an order, Meg. I know how you get when you're stuck in one spot, and we left you alone longer than I meant to this morning. I'm sorry about that, and hopefully it won't happen again. You are too valuable to be taken for granted."

I have the sudden mental image of King crouched in front of a miniature version of himself, scolding but gentle. I've seen him with children plenty of times over the years—there's a kids' surfing class every summer—but this is different. I've never so fully pictured him as a father before. And while Meg is nowhere close to being young enough to be his child, he is very clearly showing her that their relationship is far from romantic.

I've always admired his calm and careful personality, but witnessing this moment is really tugging at something deep inside me.

Something that should not be tugged.

Meg looks like she wants to argue, but she's smart. And she can probably see as well as anyone that King is nothing more than her boss. A few tears well up in her eyes, and she darts into the kitchen without a word. Suddenly looking worn down again, King takes a deep breath, letting it out slowly. Then he puts on a smile and faces the horde of customers. "Who's next?"

They erupt into chaos, all crowding forward at once and shouting questions and requests indiscriminately.

"Are you really married?"

"Can I get a dozen chocolate chip cookies?"

"Who's in charge of the bakery? You or the Yank?"

"How much for a blueberry muffin?"

King glances at me, looking rather disoriented for the first time since stepping into the bakery. He seemed so ready to handle everything that I almost forgot he admitted to being as lost as I am with this plan going forward.

I square my shoulders. We're in this together, and if I want this bakery to start to feel like mine, I'm going to have to act as such. Sticking my thumb and forefinger between my lips, I issue a shrill whistle that always worked to catch the attention of the staff in the *Home Baked* kitchens.

The bakery goes silent, all eyes turning to me. "Yes, we're really married," I say first, taking a step closer to King so I can slip my hand into his. He keeps his eyes on my face, though I feel his attention on our clasped hands, like he's trying to judge how our fingers fit together. I know he wanted to show everyone that we're married rather than talk to them, but that's not really my style. "With summer coming into full swing in a few days, we didn't want to put it off."

"But why now?" someone asks from the back. "You haven't been in Willow Cove in years."

A part of me hoped I wouldn't be remembered, but I was sorely disappointed. Pros and cons to that, I suppose. "Because I was busy filming a TV show until recently," I say. If I can manage it, I'm going to stick close to the truth with all of this. But we don't need to linger on why I'm no longer filming said TV show, so I press on. "A dozen cookies is $14.99, by the way, and muffins are $3.99, as you can see on the menu."

"Georgie is in charge of the bakery," King says before I can continue. His hand momentarily tightens around mine before he lets go and folds his arms. "Something I think y'all will be grateful for after enduring my baking for the last few months. Georgie is world class."

Whether or not he means that, I feel the praise down to my toes.

"But where is she living?" someone asks.

I wish I knew who it was so I could glare at them. What does that matter? "With my husband, obviously." Thank goodness I never got a hotel room, since I'm sure someone working at the Coralberry Cottages would have been sure to spread that info around if I had.

"Are there any other questions about our personal lives, or can we get this line moving along?" King asks. Some of the growl has returned to his voice, his expression harder than it was a moment ago. "If you're going to order something, great. If not, I'd appreciate it if you step to the side and make some space for paying customers."

An older woman near the front of the crowd raises her hand, her eyes darting between the two of us before resting on me. "Will you be making those raspberry danishes you had on the show?"

I perk up. *That's* my kind of question. "I can if you want me to. They're not on the Kingston menu, but—"

"What about those eclairs with the cherry center?" someone else asks. "Those looked amazing."

Before I know it, someone has produced a piece of paper and a pen, and people are writing down their requests of things they want me to make here at the bakery. While I'm thrilled to be able to put my talents to use beyond cookies and cupcakes, I can't help but notice the way King slowly deflates with each new request. The way he looks up at the handwritten menu that has been relatively the same for the last twenty-five years.

The way he doesn't look at me for the rest of the afternoon.

Chapter Ten

King

A SCREAM PULLS ME out of bed with a jolt, and though I try to grasp at the details of the dream I'd been having, they slip away like smoke through my fingers. It's still dark, and a part of me wonders if the scream was in my dream as I gaze blearily around my quiet bedroom.

Then I hear the whimper.

Fully awake now, I scramble out of the room and through the back door to find Georgie crouched in a ball near the pool, her arms over her head and a stream of muttered curses spilling from her lips. The sky is an inky black, but there's enough light coming from the open door of the pool house for me to see the cause of her distress.

Prince Harry is smelling her hair with great interest.

I release the tension from my shoulders with a breath. "What are you doing?"

Georgie's head snaps up, knocking into Prince Harry's mouth, and then she cowers again. "Get this monster away from me," she hisses.

I reply through a massive yawn. "You must smell good."

"*King.*"

One step forward is enough to convince the llama that his freedom is in jeopardy. Abandoning his sniffing, he lumbers quickly toward the pool. I shout and leap forward, but he's too fast for me and plunges into the dark water with a *kerplunk.*

I curse and stuff a hand into my hair. "Stupid beast," I mutter.

Standing, Georgie hurries to my side but stops about a foot away when she seems to realize I'm in nothing but my boxers. Though she averts her gaze, her blush is still obvious in the dim light. "Can, uh, can llamas swim?"

I press a hand over my heart to try to calm its racing. I think my dream had been a nice one, whatever it was. I also think Georgie might have been in it, so maybe it's a good thing she interrupted it. "Yes, they can swim. Whether they can float is another question."

Prince Harry lets out a mournful cry when he realizes his feet can't touch the bottom of the pool. A few feet to the left, and he'd be fine...

"How does he keep getting out?" I ask under my breath, moving over to the pen and the wide open gate. Even I can barely get the latch open half the time, so I really have no idea how an animal with a clear lack of opposable thumbs has managed it more times than I can count.

"Why don't you just wire it shut?" Georgie asks.

I turn to explain to her Prince Harry's bizarre need for a walk around the neighborhood every couple of days but stop when my eyes catch on what *she's* wearing. A tank top snugly hugs her curves, and her shorts could never be accused of being long. The sight of her legs—the sight of all of her, really—traps any words I might have said in my throat, leaving me standing here like an idiot with my mouth gaping open. Georgie is all woman, and I have never been gladder that I'm forcing her to sleep in the pool house.

Only the sounds of Prince Harry's splashing and complaining fill the space between us for a long few moments, until Georgie clears her throat and wraps her arms around her middle.

"Um. Does he need help, or...?"

I glance at the llama, who has begun doing laps side to side. If he would turn ninety degrees, he would discover a whole other side of the pool that he could enjoy. "He's fine. For now." I'm tempted to jump in and force him out anyway, if only for the shock of cold water to keep my thoughts where they are safe. I may need to make a few more rules if I'm going to make it through this marriage. No tank tops. No shorts. No early morning wakeups when I'm too tired to keep my eyes from studying her face. And everything else. "What time is it?"

She looks at her watch. "Three."

A laugh escapes out of my lungs. I'm used to waking up early, and bakers tend to keep early hours. But this is Willow Cove, and this town tends to sleep in. Kingston's doesn't even open until eight. "*Why?*" I breathe.

She shrugs. "I was slee..." She stops, seems to consider what she wants to say, and then shakes her head. "I couldn't sleep, so I thought I would get an early start today. But then this *creature*"—she nods toward Prince Harry—"decided he wanted to take a bite of my hair."

"Llamas don't eat hair."

"Yours seems to."

I lift my eyes to her head, which is a safer place to look anyway, and barely hold back a wince when I see a giant glob of slobber in her damp curls. At the same moment, a breeze picks up, and I get a whiff of her shampoo. My body tenses up as I resist the urge to step forward and get a deeper lungful of the tantalizing scent. She smells *amazing*, and I would love to bury my face in her hair and breathe her in. Kiss her like I did in the bakery. Maybe...

I dive into the pool before I get any bad ideas.

It takes a good twenty minutes to coax Prince Harry up the stairs on the far end and out of the pool, and neither of us are happy when I shove him back into the pen and triple check that the latch is closed. I'm soaked, I smell of wet llama again, and my early morning wakeup is starting to catch up to me; the only reason I'm not in a foul mood is because I can probably go back to sleep for a couple more hours now that Georgie is around to handle the bakery. I haven't had that luxury in weeks.

"Will it hold?"

I jump at the sound of Georgie's voice, crashing into the wire fencing with a soft curse. "I thought you were gone," I gasp.

She twists her lips up in a smirk. "And miss watching that show? I never would have guessed a llama would be so intent on staying in a pool."

I brush my hand through my hair to keep it out of my face, all too aware of Georgie's eyes tracking the movement with unveiled interest. She really needs to stop looking at me like that. I fold my arms, trying to cover some of myself up. "He loved the pool at Uncle Bill's, but mine is too deep for him. It's a miracle he hasn't drowned yet."

"Why don't you drain some of the water out so it isn't so deep?"

Her question hits me hard. Too hard. The solution is so simple, but it never once crossed my mind because I've been so tied up trying to keep everything else afloat along with Prince Harry. To my shock and horror, tears well up in my eyes, like all the emotion I've been tamping down is finally pushing back against my efforts.

I hate that Georgie is the only thing that's been able to save me from drowning when she's the one who pushed me in in the first place.

I clear my throat and turn toward the house. "That's a good idea." By some miracle, my voice comes out clear and calm. "Uh, I've got a family coming in for surf lessons today, so I probably won't be able to stop by the bakery."

"I can come by when I'm off." Georgie's voice sounds smaller than normal. "King, are you—"

"It might be a couple of busy days, honestly, so we'll have to find some way to make sure people know we're really married. I'll, uh, text you."

I slip inside the house and don't stop moving until I'm safe in my bedroom, but even then I feel like Georgie's eyes are on me. I know I shouldn't hide from her like this, not when I need to play the part of loving husband, but I'm already getting sucked into her pull, imagining how much better my life could be with her in it.

If only I knew she could stay.

To make it through this, I'm going to have to change my strategy and avoid her whenever I can. This marriage is going to be the biggest wave I've ever attempted, and to make sure I don't wipe out, I'm going to have to find my balance and ride this wave all the way through.

"Will you stop staring at me like that?" The question comes out of me rougher than I'd like, but I can't help it. This is the first time I've gone out with the guys in weeks, and they've been looking at me like I've grown a second head. "What is with y'all?"

Coop snorts a laugh. "Don't even pretend you don't know what you did, Kingston."

I sigh, gritting my teeth as the sounds of billiards and darts in the pool hall fill in the silence left behind by Coop's comment. I came out to The Shallow End, Willow Cove's local hangout spot, to try to get *away* from my new marriage, but of course my friends aren't going to ignore the elephant in the room. That would be too convenient.

"So it's true?" Duke asks, lifting an eyebrow at me. "You really married What's-her-face?"

"Georgie," Perry grunts, lining up his shot.

Beck frowns as Perry knocks two balls into the pockets at once. "Isn't she the one who always got you into trouble over the summer?"

"She's the one who turns King into a flat-out moron whenever he's around her," Coop says before I can argue. "Put the two together, and there's one brain cell between them."

I shoot a glare at him, but it isn't all that effective because the other guys laugh. These guys have known me my whole life, which I would have thought would put them on my side, but apparently not. "Pretty sure you're overreacting, Coop," I say and then turn to Beck. "I didn't get into that much trouble."

"You once stole Carl Pinnock's boat because Georgie wanted to re-enact that scene from *Tangled*," he argues.

"One of the lanterns set fire to part of the boardwalk," Duke adds.

"And almost got my dad's plane," Coop says.

I glance at Perry, wondering if he has his own addition to this attack, but he's busy planning out his next shot. Hopefully that means I'll have at least one ally tonight. The problem, though, is I can't say anything about the *Tangled* incident because it was *my* idea. Not Georgie's. "This isn't a big deal," I mumble. "So I got married. It's not going to change anything."

I'm met with four deadpan stares.

I guess I can't blame them for disagreeing with me. They're all as single as I was up until three days ago when I said, "I do," and that's unlikely to change. Clenching my hand into a fist, I shake my head and try to focus on Perry's attempt to get another striped ball.

Coop doesn't let me. "Dude, it's like you forgot how this girl broke your heart."

Duke and Beck both murmur agreement, and Perry makes his shot. He misses. Then he looks at me, and I feel like he's trying to tell me something but I don't know what it is. It would be helpful if he used his words more often than he does.

"I didn't forget," I say, trying to look at each of them so they know I mean it. "I don't think I could ever forget."

"Good," Duke says. "Because you were the worst after she left."

Beck chuckles. "I've never seen a guy mope the way you did."

Again, I can't argue, and I'm regretting more and more my decision to come out tonight. But if I had stayed home, I don't think I would have been able to avoid Georgie. I've been doing my best to keep my distance the last couple of days after the incident with Prince Harry, but each night it gets harder. I've found myself staring out the window into the backyard, hoping for a glimpse of her.

I got one earlier tonight. She was talking to her phone—a video call, probably—and pacing along the edge of the pool in a t-shirt and cutoff jean shorts, her hair pulled up in a high ponytail that spilled her curls up and out like the top of a pineapple. I had a hand on the back door before I caught myself, and I was out the front door and driving into town a moment later.

With the way the guys are looking at me, I might have been better off facing my attraction to Georgie than dealing with their judgment.

"She called me, you know," Beck says, raising his eyebrows as he watches my reaction.

I try not to clench my jaw and glare at him, though I'm not sure I succeed. "Did she?"

"Seems she has plans to renovate your uncle's bakery and needs a contractor."

"Yep." My voice breaks on that one, and I clear my throat. "Whose turn is it? Mine?"

Coop pokes me in the gut with his cue. "You're sitting out this round, dude." Then he nods for Beck to take his turn.

Chuckling, Beck bends down to try to knock the solid blue into the side pocket. "Are you good with that? Making changes?"

"The bakery is hers." Or, it will be if we can manage to get Vanderman to believe she's really my wife. Our meeting with him is tomorrow, and I keep getting more and more nervous about that. If he sees through our ruse and decides I'm trying to dupe him, what then? I could divorce Georgie and tell her we gave it our best shot, but that feels...wrong.

But it's not like these first few days of our marriage have been *right*.

"I'm meeting with her in a couple of days," Beck continues. "I can fill you in on whatever she's thinking."

"Why would I need that?"

Beck's shot is off, but only barely, and he chuckles again as he steps aside to let Coop analyze the table. "Because you looked like I slapped you when I said she called me."

That wasn't because of the renovations, but I can't tell him that. It's dangerous enough that Coop knows the truth, and while I trust my friends, I'm not sure I can trust their reactions if I tell them that my marriage to Georgie isn't real.

I shouldn't be worried that Georgie might take one look at Beck and realize she could have done better than me, but I am. Which is crazy. Our marriage is temporary, and we both know it, so it shouldn't matter if Georgie takes an interest in someone else. Maybe I'm worried about Beck's emotional stability, since he will get the same treatment I did if he tries convincing Georgie to stick around.

Though, if anyone could get her to change her mind, he probably could.

I growl a little and fold my arms, silently telling myself to relax and stop thinking about what Georgie may or may not do. I've never been able to control her actions, and I never will.

"Why marriage?" Perry asks suddenly. He speaks at the same time Coop takes his shot, which throws him off and sends the cue ball spiraling across the table.

"Dude!" Coop complains.

My gaze jumps to Perry once the ball stops moving. "What?"

He shrugs. "You haven't seen Georgie in years."

When he doesn't elaborate, Duke does it for him. "Didn't she just come back into town? Getting married is kind of skipping a few steps, especially after what happened way back when."

I glance at Coop, who narrows his eyes at me. Guess I won't be getting any help from him on this one. I shrug. "Seemed like the best thing to do at the time."

Coop barks out a laugh. "One brain cell," he repeats and pats Duke on the back, telling him to take his shot.

"Will you stop?" I complain.

"He has a point," Beck says. "Whenever you and Georgie were together, you tended to jump right into things without thinking them through first."

I force out a laugh. "As if all of you were totally logical all the time. We were *teens*. Of course we were impulsive."

"The two of you were worse," Perry says. And then, almost too quietly for me to hear, he adds, "Seems little has changed."

"Look," I say sharply, "maybe it was impulsive, but Georgie and I are married. That's not going to change." Not for a little while, anyway, but I just need them to believe me *for now*. "We've both grown up, and it is what it is. Okay?"

"How romantic," Coop mutters, rolling his eyes at me.

We're all silent for a few minutes, and the guys each take their turn until Perry is left with the eight ball and a difficult shot. But he'll probably make it. Beck must sense that he and Duke are about to lose because he turns his attention to the rest of the pool hall. There's a group of women in the corner, and though I've noticed them looking our way for the last several minutes, I've been ignoring them.

Beck seems interested until his eyes shift to my hand where it rests on my arm. "Any reason you're not wearing a ring, Kingston?" he asks. "Because we seem to have caught some attention, and I'm getting the impression they think you're available like the rest of us."

I groan. "I've been busy."

"Georgie doesn't have one either," Coop adds unhelpfully.

"Busy," I repeat.

"Maybe you should get unbusy and show the world you're off the market," Duke says. "Make some space for the rest of us."

Perry bounces the eight ball off the wall and into the corner pocket, just as he planned, and then he sends a searing scowl toward Duke. "Speak for yourself," he grunts.

"Amen to that," Beck agrees.

Coop turns his gaze to me, eyes narrowed but a mischievous grin on his face. "Here's hoping your fun little impulse decision doesn't prove us all right. Love is the worst, and you might be the biggest idiot of all of us for thinking otherwise."

Even if he knows my marriage is fake, I'm worried Coop is going to end up being right, just as he predicted. Love is dangerous.

And Georgie even more so.

Chapter Eleven

Georgie

I'VE BARELY SEEN KING the last few days. It's not exactly a surprise—he warned me he would be busy—but my disappointment is definitely concerning. We both agreed that we can't get attached to each other. But when a girl watches a man physically heft an animal as large as a water-laden llama out of a pool, her mind starts to get ideas. I had been annoyed that my sleepwalking pulled me out of the house in the middle of the night until King dove into the pool and gave me a show.

If I'm being honest, that morning was just a cherry on top of the ice cream sundae that is Royal Kingston. During the moments when I *have* seen him the last couple days—like when I dropped off some fresh croissants at the surf shack and watched him teach three little kids how to balance on their miniature surfboards, all four of them with broad smiles—I felt like I was getting a front row seat to the man he has become.

I liked him when we were younger. Maybe even loved him. But I never looked at him back then like I've been doing since we tied the knot.

It's dangerous.

"Mrs. Vanderman just came in," Emily says, poking her head into the kitchen.

Now that school is out, she and Meg have started switching shifts. The seventeen-year-old is not especially skilled at baking and has a lot to learn, but I haven't minded the change in company. Meg's unveiled glares were getting tiresome. I've been able to handle the morning baking on my own just fine, glad to have a chance to roam the kitchen freely without worrying about getting in someone else's way, and Meg has been helpful with prepping for the next day before she locks up in the afternoons.

It's a relief to have found a sort of rhythm together, though she still seems sad that I stole what chances she had with King, however small they were.

"Are the sticky buns ready?" Emily asks.

As I carefully fold almond flour into my egg whites for a batch of macarons, I glance at the one oven that isn't finicky, which is currently baking the sticky buns that Mrs. Vanderman is particularly fond of. "Five minutes," I tell Emily. I would have liked them to be done already, but I'm not about to serve the woman a subpar bun the morning before I convince her husband to transfer the bakery to me. Our appointment is in an hour or so, and I've been dreading it since leaving the courthouse.

Especially because Mrs. Vanderman has been here every day. King says that's normal, but the stern-looking attorney's wife seems to watch me more closely than what is socially acceptable. If I had to put money on it, she doesn't seem to think our marriage is a real one. That makes me worried to learn of her husband's opinion on the matter.

With King too busy to make appearances at the bakery, I'm using the only weapon I've got to combat Mrs. Vanderman's skepticism: exceptional sticky buns.

The bell above the front door jingles merrily as Emily heads back to the lobby, hopefully to tell Mrs. Vanderman that her breakfast will be out momentarily. We've had a pretty constant stream of customers now that summer is officially here, and I hope it continues. I've got a meeting tomorrow with a local contractor, Beck Billingsley, to see how much it will cost to do some refurbishments, and I'll need as many profits as I can get to pay for them.

I haven't had many moments of missing my life with Lane, but they tend to happen when I look at my bank account.

"Georgie?" The voice that calls from the lobby is familiar, but I can't quite place who it belongs to because I've reacquainted with a lot of people over the last few days—too many to keep track of. It never ceases to amaze me how many people remember me from all those years ago, given I was only ever here in the summers and didn't interact with many people outside of King and his friends. I guess my days spent at the bakery were more memorable than I thought.

Emily pushes through the swinging door again, a frown on her lips. "There's someone here who says she's your best friend," she says.

I can't help but grin at the way she seems to be trying to defend me. Yes, Emily is a definite step up from Meg, at least when it comes to company. "I don't really have friends in Willow Cove. Or at all," I add under my breath. Just Cecily, who is...

My grin drops as recognition sets in. Why is Cecily in South Carolina?

Setting aside my batter, I brush my hands on my apron and hurry to follow Emily out to the front. Sure enough, my best friend is standing on the other side of the counter, her arms folded and a look of unadulterated frustration on her face.

As soon as she sees me, however, her scowl shifts into a wide grin. "You're alive!"

I skirt around the counter and attack her with a fierce hug. "I talked to you last night." The words come out tinged with emotion. Apparently I missed my friend more than I realized. Video chats aren't the same as seeing her in person. "I can't believe you're here!"

Cecily snorts. "I only missed your wedding because you neglected to tell me about it beforehand. Otherwise I would have been here sooner."

I glance at Mrs. Vanderman, who narrows her eyes at me, and then I take hold of Cecily's hand so I can tug her into the kitchen. It's not completely private, but it's better than having a conversation like this in the middle of the busy lobby.

"You'd better keep your voice down," I warn her. "We're meeting with the estate attorney this afternoon, and his wife is out there."

Cecily raises an eyebrow. "Okay?" I filled her in on the whole situation the night after I married King, but she's clearly not grasping my warning.

I sigh and grab a pastry bag so I can start piping the macarons, though I fill the bag half-heartedly. I'm worried this batch is going to fail like the last one; Willow Cove is more humid than Manhattan was, and the little cookies are finicky to begin with. I need to play with them more and adjust my ratios, but they feel like a metaphor for how much I've been failing at life lately.

"I think she suspects there's something fishy about my marriage to King," I mutter.

Cecily hops onto an empty spot of counter and sticks her finger in a bowl of cookie dough, taking a swipe and sticking it in her mouth. I resist the urge to groan now that that batch is unusable. "In case you've forgotten, there *is* something fishy about your marriage. When do I get to meet this questionable husband of yours, anyway?"

I keep my eyes on the baking sheet I'm piping onto. "Hopefully never?"

She gasps. "Rude! And to think I came all this way to help make sure the two of you are a solid couple." She sounds too put out for her disappointment to be real, but I glare at her anyway, in part because she's wrong and because she's really struggling with keeping her voice down.

Glancing around the kitchen, I turn on the mixer that I used to whip my egg whites, hoping the whirring will cover our conversation so no one up front hears. "We're not solid," I argue. "And that's a good thing."

"Not if you want your marriage to last."

"Which I don't," I remind her. I went on a whole rant about it last night, telling her about my plan to use the profits to start something new somewhere else.

Cecily eats more cookie dough, humming with pleasure as she licks her fingers. "You know, most couples go into a marriage wanting it to last forever."

I glance at the door, as if I might be able to see Mrs. Vanderman peering through the window. "This isn't a 'most couples' situation, Cece."

"So you've said."

"King and I have history that makes this complicated."

I glance up when she doesn't say anything else and cringe when I realize she's giving me her therapist stare. I've never regretted befriending a marriage counselor more than I do right now. "What?"

She cocks her head, examining me. "Nothing."

"*What*?" I demand again.

"You didn't say much about how you and King became a couple."

I roll my eyes and finish off the last macaron, and then I tap the cookie sheet a few times to get rid of any bubbles before stashing the tray on a cart to rest. "What more is there to say? He can't give me the bakery unless I'm—"

"I mean before. Before you came to New York. It still baffles me that you kept him a secret all these years."

I can't help but wince. When I discovered the room Cecily was subleasing in her apartment when I first moved to New York, her friendship was a godsend. I was completely out of my element and already homesick, and her warm welcome gave me the courage to stick around and really try to make a life for myself in the city. We became fast friends while she went through school and I found work in a bakery, and I opened up to her in a way I haven't with anyone else.

I told her everything. Except when it came to King. The only person I've ever talked to about our past relationship is Bill, and he always seemed to understand why I left, which helped me feel like I could move on.

Sighing, I lean against the counter and keep my eyes on the floor. "I was heartbroken when I left Willow Cove. Not exactly something I wanted to revisit."

"You're the one who ended things," she reminds me.

"I know. But we were kids when he asked me to marry him. What was I supposed to do?"

"That's the question, isn't it?"

"Georgie?" Emily is back again. "Are the sticky buns ready?"

I let out a curse and dash toward the oven. The buns are a little overdone, but not unsalvageable. I dish one up and hand it to Emily. "On the house," I tell her and practically shove her back into the lobby.

Cecily snickers. "I haven't heard you use language like that since before you started dating Lane. I haven't seen you this relaxed either."

I let out a laugh that feels like it's on the verge of being maniacal. "I am not remotely relaxed," I argue, lowering my voice. "This meeting with the attorney is freaking me out."

"Why?"

I know she's doing her therapist thing and trying to dig, but I'm too nervous to resist. "Because if he doesn't think we're really married, then the bakery—"

"Why will it be so difficult to convince him? You already said you're attracted to King."

I wish I hadn't told her that part. "That doesn't mean I can pretend to be his loving wife."

Cecily shrugs. "All you have to do is bat your eyes at him and be all lovey dovey. If he was repulsive, I would understand the difficulty, but you had heart eyes when you were telling me about this hunky husband of yours."

I point a finger at her. "I never called him hunky."

"Not with your words, no. But your facial expressions?" She lets out a deep sigh, like she's about to swoon from the romance of it all. Sometimes I wonder how her husband puts up with her romantic heart, but then I remember he proposed to her in front of the Eiffel Tower. They're the most sickeningly adorable couple I know. "I'll reserve judgment until I meet the man, but I have a good feeling about you two."

I roll my eyes. "I feel like your opinions on love should disqualify you from being a marriage counselor. Real life isn't the same as fairy tales."

"I know that! It's so much better. And I know you only recently got dumped in the worst possible way, so you're allowed to be a little cynical."

"Thank you."

"For now."

I sigh. "I'm glad you're here, Cece, but you are incredibly annoying some-times, you know that?"

She grins. "I know. But Georgie, you're acting like you can control everything that's happening here, and you can't. This isn't just about you, and you're going to worry yourself into a mess if you keep living so scared of what other people might do. Not everyone is like Lane."

"Georgie!" Emily pokes her head back yet again, this time with a sparkle in her eyes. "King is here." Giving me a wide smile, she returns to the counter.

"Yay!" Cecily leaps to her feet and looks way too excited for me to feel com-fortable about what might happen next. I haven't even had a chance to process what she said before Emily interrupted. "I get to meet the pretend husband!"

"The husband part is very real," I argue right as King steps into the kitchen.

Like it does every time I see King, my heart throbs in my chest in a way that makes me think I should get it looked at. That can't be healthy.

He takes only a couple of steps into the kitchen before he sees Cecily, and then he stops dead, eyes taking her in before darting to me with a clear question in his gaze. Beyond that, there isn't much to his expression, so it's hard to know what he might be thinking.

I turn off the mixer and grip the edges of my apron, wishing I could have avoided this interaction entirely. "King, this is my friend, Cecily. Cecily, this is, uh..."

"The hunky husband," she finishes for me.

The smallest of smiles tugs on King's lips. "It's nice to meet you, Cecily." His voice is deep and rumbly, and I'm cursing the fact that he hasn't shaved in a couple of days because that dark scruff on his jaw is tantalizing, begging to be stroked. He takes another step toward us and folds his arms, offering plenty of distractions from his face. "Did she really call me hunky?"

Cecily's grin is far too wicked for me to be comfortable right now. "More or less. And what's your opinion of your new wife?"

King's eyes jump to me again, only long enough to leave a searing trail from my head to my toes. I don't know how he manages to leave a physical sensation like that without touching me, but he does. I'm blaming the fact that I've only seen him in passing this week and therefore haven't had a chance to become immune to his gaze.

"Don't answer that," Cecily says. There's laughter behind the words. "Are you here to bake with Georgie?"

"Nobody wants that," King says before I can find an excuse to get him out of my kitchen. Technically it's still his kitchen, but considering he hasn't been here in days, I'm claiming it as mine now. "Besides, Coop reminded me we should probably get some rings before our meeting today."

I look down at my bare fingers. I don't usually wear jewelry while working—getting dough out of the nooks and crannies of a ring is a nightmare—but I get a sudden and potent memory of Lane asking if I would wear a ring on the show if he gave it to me. It was an off-hand comment during one of the episodes, but it led to all sorts of speculation from our viewers. Some people even predicted Lane was going to propose to me, which started a run several episodes long that felt more like scripted reality TV than a baking show.

That was months ago. Right around the time Bill died.

"Georgie?" King says. "How are things looking here? We don't have a ton of time before our meeting, so we'd need to go now."

"Yeah," I breathe and tug my apron loose. "Yeah, we should do that while we can."

"I'll come with you!" Cecily says brightly.

I nearly groan. I really don't want her analyzing my every interaction with King, but if I tell her not to come with us, she'll read too much into that too. If I thought Cecily wouldn't come to all the wrong conclusions, I wouldn't have told her this marriage was fake in the first place.

Not that I could have lied to my best friend. The only reason I've been able to do any of this is because King and I are, technically, married, so I haven't had to lie to anyone. *Technically*.

King doesn't seem particularly thrilled about my friend inviting herself on our ring-buying excursion, and I'm pretty sure he's about to say as much, so I speak first. "That's a good idea, Cece. You'll be able to help me find a good one. Who's driving?"

"Your car scares me," King says without hesitation. "I'm driving."

Cecily laughs out loud as she tucks her arm through mine and follows King out to the front. "I'm glad it's not just me! I almost didn't let her drive away in that thing."

"My car is fine," I complain, even if they're probably right. I didn't need a car in New York, but when Lane broke up with me and kicked me out of the company, I needed something to run away in. I bought the first car I came across, which in hindsight wasn't the best idea.

"Honey." Cecily doesn't say anything else until we're halfway through the lobby, probably because she's too busy taking everything in as we walk. "I think you'd better let your husband spoil you and get you something that won't fall apart if you drive it over thirty miles per hour."

King glances back when he reaches the door but doesn't respond.

I jab my elbow into Cecily's side. "I know what you're doing," I hiss, even if that's a lie. She's the sort of person who likes to think she knows what's best for people, which in turn leads to her making decisions for those people. She didn't put up this much of a fuss about my car back in New York, no matter what she says, and she's talking far louder than necessary.

Something in the lobby sparked her comment, and my money is on Mrs. Vanderman.

When we step outside onto the boardwalk, King pauses and folds his arms without a word. Before I can ask why, someone else speaks up.

"Nice to see you're both still alive and unharmed."

I grit my teeth. "Coop."

He nods his head once, leaning against the side of the bakery and looking for all the world like a man without a care. He has the classic California surfer-boy look, with his wavy blond hair and board shorts, and from what I've heard from people coming into the bakery, he's every bit the devil-may-care guy I remember. He flies tourists around to the nearby islands, but beyond that I get the sense that he doesn't do much with his life.

Coop's eyes are full of laughter as he glances between King and me, and then he looks over at Cecily. Interest sparks to life in his expression. "Who do we have here?"

"A happily married woman," Cecily replies easily. "So keep your eyes to yourself."

"Yes, ma'am."

"Coop is coming with us," King says on a sigh.

"I thought you might need a buffer," Coop says. "Though, looks like you found one yourself."

Cecily extricates herself from my arm, somehow managing to push me into King's side at the same time she steps closer to Coop. I have to grab King's arm to keep from falling over. "What's your take on this little marriage?" she asks Coop.

He frowns and looks around to make sure there's no one to overhear our conversation. It's still early enough in the day that the boardwalk isn't overflowing with people yet. "I give it another week," he says with a chuckle.

Cecily hums thoughtfully. "Interesting."

"Can we go?" I ask, but my words falter when I realize I'm no longer holding King's arm but his hand. When did that happen?

King looks as concerned as I am, though he's smart enough to keep a hold of me now that we're holding hands. There are probably people watching us through the bakery windows, Mrs. Vanderman included, and there's no telling who else may be noticing our little conversation on the boardwalk. "Yes, we can go," he says and leads me toward the parking lot.

Neither of us look back to see if our friends are following us.

Chapter Twelve

King

"I STILL DON'T SEE why you're going to all this trouble," Coop says as he fiddles with a display of gimmicky rings, some made of seashells and some shaped like turtles, among other things.

I figured going to an actual jeweler would end with us empty-handed, given neither Georgie nor I want to spend a lot of money on these rings, so I picked a tourist shop not far from one of the many Willow Cove beaches. They have some nice stuff, but there's also a lot of cheesy options like the ones Coop is playing with.

I sigh and glance across the store to where Georgie and her friend are deep in conversation while they peruse a shelf full of little trinkets. I'm not sure what to make of Cecily, but Georgie seems a lot happier than she has the last couple of days. Not that I've seen her often enough to really make a judgment call on her happiness, but she's not the sort of person who can hide what she's feeling.

Her smile hasn't been completely real since the morning Prince Harry escaped.

My heart throbs in my chest, the same thing it's done every time I've seen my temporary wife. Turns out avoiding her has done nothing to curb my returning feelings for her, and I'm going to have to come up with another strategy for survival. I'm pretty sure being away from her has only made things worse.

"We have to make sure Vanderman thinks we're in this for good," I tell Coop. "Rings will make it all seem more authentic." I blamed this excursion on Coop, but I haven't been able to stop thinking about getting Georgie a ring since Beck mentioned it last night at the pool hall.

Coop slips a turtle ring onto his little finger and holds it up to admire it. "Why didn't you just give her the ring you bought ten years ago? I know you still have it."

A jolt of terror spurs me forward, and I clap a hand over his mouth as if that might stop him from saying what he just said. Georgie and Cecily look over in curiosity, but I ignore them as Coop tries to struggle out of my hold. "How do you know that?" I hiss.

We scuffle until he gets himself free and scowls at me. "I don't need to breathe. It's fine."

"Answer the question, Heyes."

"Because I helped you move into your house, you moron." He straightens his t-shirt and pushes his hair out of his face. "And I might have rifled through your underwear drawer a time or two."

I groan. "Why do I put up with you?"

"Because you and I are the same, man. We'd be alone without each other."

Rolling my eyes, I start searching through a nicer array of rings, hoping to find something that Georgie might like. It's not like I know her well enough for that. She doesn't *seem* all that different from the girl I knew, but I know I've changed a lot over the last ten years. I'm sure she has too. "Still not interested in dating?"

"Why would I willingly subject myself to torture? I've got plenty to keep me occupied."

I know Coop's dad has been sick, leaving more of the business to Coop, but I doubt there aren't moments when he wishes for more than just work. Then again, perpetual singleness seems to be the theme of the guys of Willow Cove. "Do you ever get tired of flying tourists around?" I ask, running my finger along the many ring options.

Coop tugs on the ring he put on his pinky and shrugs. "Nah. Plus, I get to fly an irritating turtle nut around for a couple of weeks, which is going to be..." He shudders. "So much fun." He tugs on the ring again, his eyebrows dropping lower.

Leave it to Coop to get a cheap ring stuck on his finger.

Sighing, I pick up a ring that has a bit of sea glass in the setting in place of a precious stone and look at it more closely. "How's your dad?"

"Nope."

I'm not surprised when he wanders off after that blunt response, which is partly why I asked. He hates talking about anything personal, and there's nothing more personal than his dad. Plus, he seems determined to free himself from the too-small ring, so that will keep him occupied for a while and give me a chance to do what I came here to do.

With the sea glass ring in hand, I move to the other side of the store and approach Georgie slowly. It's as much because I don't want to interrupt her conversation as it is because I don't like the way Cecily looks at me. I know nothing about her, but I get the feeling she sees more than the average person.

Sure enough, Cecily is the first to notice me, and the look in her eyes is sharp and calculating. "Find something?" she asks.

Georgie turns around, and her eyes drop to the ring pinched between my fingers. "Oh, that's beautiful!" When her fingers brush against mine as she grabs the ring, I feel her touch deep in my chest.

"What is that, jade?" Cecily asks.

"Sea glass," Georgie and I say at the same time.

I meet her gaze, hating how much her smile warms me. Maybe avoiding her was my best option after all because now that I'm standing next to her, I don't want to leave.

Why is this so difficult?

Her tongue darts across her lips, the movement holding my attention completely, and then she turns to give her friend a closer look at the translucent green ring. "I used to love walking on the beach collecting bits of sea glass," she says. There's a fondness in her voice that sparks memories of doing that very thing with her.

I don't especially have an interest in the smooth glass pebbles, but I always liked the way Georgie found them fascinating. I kept trying to find one that matched the color of her eyes, but I never did. I still find myself searching the sand sometimes without meaning to.

"Interesting," Cecily says, glancing from the ring to Georgie to me.

Georgie scowls. "Don't go analyzing us, Cece. I don't need your marriage counselor ways making this whole thing more complicated than it already is."

Ah, that's why she's so observant. Suddenly I feel like I need to keep on my guard when I'm around Cecily. "How long are you in town, Cecily?" I know the question is out of left field, but it's an important bit of information I need for my sanity.

She gives me a sweet smile. "That depends."

"On what?"

"Ow!" There's a bang as Coop shouts, pulling all our attention to the other side of the shop where he seems to be attempting to use gravity to pull the ring free. I'm not sure how jumping is supposed to help him, and it looks like he's already crashed into the hat display next to him.

"Is he okay?" Cecily asks.

I shrug. "He got stuck in a turtle ring."

"Does he need help?" Georgie asks.

"Probably. Does it fit?" I nod toward the ring she's holding.

Georgie slips the ring onto her left ring finger and holds it up so it catches the light. A knot forms in my stomach when I notice how similar the green color is to her eyes. Far closer than anything I found back then, though it's not an exact match. I doubt there's anything in the world that can match the vibrant color of her eyes. They're as unique as she is.

Cecily clears her throat.

"Yes!" Georgie drops her hand, her cheeks blossoming with pink. "Yes, it fits."

I smile. "Good."

"Oh, for heaven's sake." Sighing with exasperation, Cecily pulls a bottle of lotion out of her purse and then stomps across the store to Coop, leaving me alone with Georgie.

I'm both annoyed and grateful.

"I found one for you too," Georgie says and gives me a thumbs up. It takes me a second to realize it's because she's wearing the ring on her thumb. It's a silver band with a wave etched into the metal. "It's kind of cheesy, but I figured we could use all the cheese we can get to sell this thing."

Before I can say anything, she grabs hold of my left hand and slides the ring on for me. Surprisingly, it fits decently well. I'll have to be sure to leave it in the office before I take students out to the surf so it doesn't slip off in the water. I have a sudden, heart-gripping fear that I'll lose the stupid thing within hours of Georgie giving it to me.

"It's dumb," she says and goes to pull it off again.

I grab her hand to stop her. "I like it." Just like how I like holding her hand. Her skin is soft beneath the pads of my fingers, though a bit dry because she has to wash them so often when baking. I should pick up some lotion for the bakery. I don't know if she is the sort to need one of the super fancy kinds that can only be found in specialty stores in the city, but regardless, I should get her something. These hands can work miracles in a kitchen, and they deserve to be cared for as much as the rest of her does.

"King," Georgie whispers, pulling my eyes from her hands to her face. Her gaze is hooded. Wary. But there's plenty of desire in there for me to know it's not just me who hasn't liked the last couple of days of being apart.

"You're going to leave," I remind myself out loud.

"And you never will," she says in turn.

Our hands slip apart as we simultaneously turn to see if Cecily has managed to free Coop from his predicament.

In the end, we leave the store with three rings. Mine, Georgie's, and the one that is currently cutting off Coop's circulation.

Chapter Thirteen

Georgie

"I MUST SAY, THIS is all very irregular." Mr. Vanderman squints at us from behind his bifocals before looking back down at the large stack of papers in his hands.

He's pretty much been saying variations of that same thing for the last twenty minutes, and every time he does, I get a little more nervous. If I can't get my name added to the deed for the bakery, this marriage will have been for nothing. No wonder King stressed our need to make our marriage look legit.

King's hand tightens around mine as he shifts a bit in his seat. "Uncle Bill always talked about how he wanted Georgie to have the bakery."

"Then he should have left it to her," Mr. Vanderman mutters to himself. He holds one sheet of paper closer to his face, hiding himself from view as he reads it.

King frowns, but there's something in his expression that speaks of resignation. If he's already willing to give up, we're going to have a problem.

I sit forward. "Mr. Vanderman, Bill must have known King and I were going to end up here eventually, but he wasn't sure when I would be coming back to Willow Cove. He probably thought it was safer if he left it to—"

"His family, Miss Carpenter." Mr. Vanderman peers at me over the top of the paper. "I've noticed you haven't applied to change your name yet."

Of course he would point that out. I look at King, who doesn't look back. We already had this discussion, but I don't think the stuffy attorney will accept "it sounds funny" as a suitable reason to keep my maiden name over Kingston. I scramble for some other excuse. "Carpenter is my professional name, and the one I'm known by in the baking world. For the sake of the bakery, I thought I should keep it."

"Hmm." Mr. Vanderman purses his lips as he looks between us.

"Besides, she'd basically be named King George," Coop says behind us. Honestly, I'm not sure how he and Cecily managed to end up in the room to witness this awkward conversation, but the two of them are sitting in the back of the office with opposite expressions. Coop looks like he would rather be anywhere but here, and Cecily has some mischief in her eyes that I really don't like. She's been looking at me like that ever since we left the tourist shop, though she's been surprisingly mum.

"Mr. Heyes, you are here as an unnecessary witness, not to offer your opinions." Placing the paper on the desk, Mr. Vanderman looks at each of us in turn before fixing his hard gaze on King. "Mr. Kingston, you are aware that I considered your uncle a dear friend before he departed this world, and as such I know precisely why he chose to leave his legacy to you rather than an outsider."

I may not be a Willow Cove native, but I've spent enough time in this town to be more than an outsider. I'm about to say as much when King takes my hand and squeezes. I'm not sure if it's reassurance or a warning, but I reluctantly keep my mouth shut.

"Uncle Bill wanted his bakery to thrive," King says slowly. "He knew I wouldn't let him down if something happened to him."

"Exactly."

"And I think the best thing for that bakery is for Georgie to have it."

Mr. Vanderman purses his lips and turns his gaze to me. I don't know what it is about him, but something about the way he looks at me feels almost painful. "I did not see you at the funeral, Miss Carpenter."

Before I can say a word, King growls out, "That's *Mrs.* Carpenter, sir. Whether you believe it or not, she's my wife."

She's my wife. I've been reading too many romance novels because those few words send a shiver through me.

Cecily snickers. I really hope she didn't see that shiver.

Mr. Vanderman scoffs, glancing between us before fixing his steely eyes on me once more. "Mrs. Carpenter, despite your absence over the last several years, you have certainly taken a shine to your new role in this family quickly, what with all the changes you're making to the bakery menu. It's not yours yet."

Why in the world is this guy so against scribbling my name onto a piece of paper? My goodness, it's like he's angry on King's behalf for the way I left. "What does a menu have to do with my marriage?" I ask sharply. "The people of Willow Cove have been requesting all of that stuff, so it's not like—"

"And I have heard you will be employing Mr. Billingsley to make extensive renovations," Mr. Vanderman continues.

King's hand tightens around mine.

"I don't know if I would call them extensive," I argue. I haven't even met with Beck yet. "But the place does need updating if we want it to—"

"Now that you are married, I don't see why you cannot carry on as you are doing without bothering with the arduous process of changing ownership."

My stomach drops. I knew he was going to be hesitant, based on what King said the day before we got married, but if he thinks I should be content to do everything in my husband's name, I'm not sure I'm going to be able to last long. Yes, I can revive the bakery without being the owner, but I can't spend the rest of my life having to ask permission to do anything. I won't be able to go start my own bakery somewhere else without King needing to come with me to sign all the paperwork because everything will be in his name, including the profits I would use as a down payment. Never mind my independence; I can't ask that of King.

He deserves more than that.

Besides, the last time I trusted my livelihood to someone else's name, it left me with nothing. *Lane* left me with nothing. King isn't that kind of man, but that wound is going to be raw for a long time.

"With all due respect," I say carefully, "that sounds incredibly old-fashioned and misogynistic, Mr. Vanderman."

He sniffs. "I don't see how—"

"You're expecting me to put my blood, sweat, and tears into *my husband's* business so *he* can enjoy the benefits. So *his* net worth can increase. You are aware that, even when married, we have our own credit scores and financial histories. We are individual people regardless of our marital status. King is too busy with his own business to have to be at my beck and call while I try to rescue Bill's legacy from falling to ruin under King's hand."

I grimace and send an apologetic look at King, only to find him with a little smile as he looks back at me.

"She's right," he says. "The place has been falling apart ever since Uncle Bill passed, and I'm no good at baking. I don't even want..." His words fall off for a second before he chokes out the last few words. "Don't want the bakery." That was a lie.

I know he's holding on to the last bit of his family, and I hope I can make all the changes I need to without him feeling like he's lost the last of the Kingstons. Even when I go somewhere else to start my own thing, I won't abandon Kingston's Bakery. It'll live on in Willow Cove forever, just with someone else in the kitchen.

"Hmm." Mr. Vanderman glances between us, his expression more irritated than thoughtful. "Well, I confess I am still wary of this arrangement. Your marriage, so quickly settled, has raised a good number of questions."

"Such as?" I ask.

"Were you not in a relationship with one..." He squints down at one of his pieces of paper. "...Lane Beretto until quite recently?"

My stomach twists, leaving me slightly nauseous. I won't be able to answer his question honestly without things looking questionable, and I don't like the idea of lying. But I have to say something. "My relationship with Lane was a product of the TV show, Mr. Vanderman."

"Be that as it may, its recent nature still calls into question the strength of *this* union and its likelihood of surviving." Not one to mince words, Mr. V.

Coop snorts a little laugh, which I don't appreciate, but it's King who speaks up. "What are you insinuating?" he growls, sitting up a little straighter.

Mr. Vanderman's lips curl up in the slightest of smiles. "I am only suggesting Miss Carpenter—"

"Mrs."

"—has a history of flightiness that speaks of an inability to commit to more than—"

"That's enough!" King jumps to his feet, and I'm glad I'm still gripping his hand because otherwise he might actually throw a punch. "Mr. Vanderman, I'm going to ask you one time to stop speaking to my wife like that. If you're incapable of being professional, maybe it's time for you to retire. I am more than happy to hire a new attorney to handle the estate, and the only reason I've kept you is because you were Uncle Bill's friend." He looks down his nose at the old man. "Can't see why, though."

I know this moment is serious and that I should be incredibly offended by the way Vanderman is treating me, and I am. *But good glory my husband is attractive.* I don't think I've ever had a man defend me the way King did just now, and my whole body is buzzing as I stare up at his clenched jaw and fiery eyes. If Lane had ever done that on the show, our ratings would have shot up like crazy.

Someone clears their throat behind us, and it takes me a second to realize it's Cecily. She has a hand in the air and an excited smile on her face. "If I may offer a suggestion," she says to Mr. Vanderman.

The attorney, who turned a healthy shade of red when King shouted at him, narrows his eyes. "What?" he snaps.

Cecily isn't bothered by his incivility. "Maybe, given the circumstances of their quick engagement and subsequent nuptials, Mr. Kingston and Mrs. Carpenter might benefit from the services of a marriage counselor?"

The blood rushes from my face, leaving me dizzy. What is she doing?

King snarls a little. "We're fine. I don't think we need—"

"Oh, counseling is beneficial for couples of all dispositions," Cecily says to him. She's put on her serious therapist voice, which is so different from her usual bubbly personality that it always catches me off guard when I hear it. "Even the strongest of marriages have found advantages in having an objective third party involved in keeping their relationship on a solid foundation." She looks at Mr. Vanderman again. "I would be happy to offer my assistance as you ascertain the viability of transferring ownership from husband to wife."

Coop scoffs, one eyebrow raised high. I honestly can't tell if he thinks my friend is insane or a genius. I'm wondering the same thing myself.

"I think a week or two of observation and facilitated conversation with a licensed professional could ease your mind on the matter," Cecily continues, and then she hurries forward to hand the attorney her card, smashing herself between the two of us.

I grip King's hand tighter, in case he thinks of letting go now that Cecily is inserting herself into our lives and leaning against our arms. Right now, I need to know we're in this together; it will be a whole lot easier to murder my best friend if I have an accomplice.

Mr. Vanderman stares at the card for a long while, his thoughts practically visible behind his eyes, and then he lifts a cold gaze to King. "You will understand that I only want to follow William Kingston's wishes on this matter."

King grows even more tense than before.

"But..." Mr. Vanderman sighs. "I suppose I have no legitimate reasons to claim your marriage is not going to last. I am not a prophet. If you will agree to two weeks of observation"—he eyes Cecily with suspicion—"with a professional I will choose for you, then—"

"No." I swallow, feeling four sets of eyes on me. "I will talk to Dr. Preston, but anyone from Willow Cove will have bias in the matter."

"Dr. Preston is your friend," Mr. Vanderman argues with a roll of his eyes. "If anyone is going to have bias..."

I shake my head, pleased when Cecily keeps her expression firm. "No, see, Cecily wants me to move back to New York where she is, so if she says my marriage to King is sound, you'll know she means it. And if she doesn't, then you'll all win. But this marriage is real, so it doesn't matter." It's real, but that doesn't mean it's lasting.

King's expression is hard to see with Cecily standing between us, but I feel his reaction to my words in the twitch of his hand. I wish I knew what it meant.

"I do want her to move back," Cecily allows. "But I am also firmly professional when it comes to my occupation. If Mr. Kingston is also agreeable to my services, free of charge, of course, as this would not be official counseling due to my relationship with Mrs. Carpenter, then may we proceed?"

Mr. Vanderman looks like he wants to keep arguing, but I think he's smart enough to know King will likely follow through with his threat and find another attorney to handle our case. I'm pretty sure the only reason King is still willing to work with Vanderman in the first place is because of his friendship with Bill, but that loyalty is waning.

Mr. Vanderman sighs heavily. "Very well. We will reconvene in two weeks, and if Dr. Preston's report deems this relationship to be healthy and lasting, then we can proceed with our discussions."

He's not specifically saying he'll transfer the bakery to me, but I think this is as good as I'll get from this guy. I don't love the idea of spending two more weeks in a marriage with King while there's still the possibility that it will be for nothing, but I didn't come into this thinking it was a guarantee. I can handle a few challenges.

Cecily turns to King. "Well, Kingston? Think you can survive a couple of weeks of counseling with your wife's most favorite person?"

She's pushing buttons because that's what she does, and I'm not sure that's a good idea when it comes to King. He has been more relaxed since the first day I arrived in Willow Cove now that he's not worried about the bakery, but he's certainly tense enough right now to snap at her like he did Mr. Vanderman.

To my shock and relief, King leans around Cecily to smile at me. "I thought I was your favorite person."

I can't help but smile back at him. "It's a toss-up. Cecily used to make me smoothies every morning."

"That's a tough act to follow."

"I'm sure you'll think of something."

"Are we done now?" Coop asks, interrupting our back-and-forth. "Some of us have jobs. Including the two of you. Jury's out on Princess Shrink and her fancy doctorate."

Scoffing, Cecily grabs hold of my hand, which is still clinging to King's, and tugs us toward the door. "Anyone with a real job has the ability to take a vacation."

Coop barks out a laugh as he follows us out the exit. "I have a real job."

"I will believe that when I see it, Mr. Heyes."

"How soon before you go back to New York?"

"No one says you have to hang around while I'm in town."

"King's my best friend. I'm not about to—"

"Will you two stop?" I snap that question at the same time King growls low in his throat, so I know he's as annoyed as I am. At this point, we've made it out into the little parking lot outside Mr. Vanderman's office and are alone, which is nice. I don't have to feel like I'm under scrutiny for now. "It's going to be hard enough to get through this marriage as it is, and we don't need you going after each other's throats."

Cecily ducks her head sheepishly, and Coop simply gives King a nod and folds his arms.

I let out a deep breath. "Thank you. Cece, what in the world was that?"

She blinks, though she doesn't look as innocent as I'm sure she would like to. "What was what?"

"We don't have time for marriage counseling," King replies.

"I'm more than happy to work around your schedules."

King and I share a glance, likely thinking the same thing. "You know you don't have to actually have any sessions with us, right?" I point out. "You can tell Mr. Vanderman that—"

"Georgiana Tiara Carpenter!" Cecily points a finger at me and looks genuinely angry. "I am not about to lie for you and besmirch my well-respected reputation just because you don't think you can hack a real marriage."

Coop snickers. When I glare at him, he shrugs. "I'm not laughing at Miss High-and-Mighty."

"That's Mrs. High-and-Mighty to you," Cecily says.

"Whatever. I'm laughing because your middle name is Tiara."

I narrow my eyes. "What of it?"

"Nothing at all."

But it's not nothing because King's hand tightens once more around mine, and he's looking at me with a curious look in his eyes. "I don't think I knew your middle name."

Whatever thoughts are going through his head, the expression they're giving him is making me squirm. "You never needed to know it," I mutter.

"Agree to disagree," he mutters back. "Cecily, I know you were trying to help, but we really don't have time to—"

"Like I said." Cecily fixes on her therapist stare, which is enough to make me shrink into King's side in fear of what might be awaiting us in the next two weeks. "I gave that obnoxious attorney my word that I would do this right, so that's what I'm going to do. You will give me your schedules, and I will find times that work for both of you." She looks specifically at me. "If you want that bakery, and I know you do, you'll cooperate."

I want to argue, but I don't. "Fine."

"And you." She looks at King. "You will be open and honest, no matter how uncomfortable you might be. The goal of this is to talk things through and clear some air so Mr. Vanderman knows you are both trying to make this work, even if it is only for a short time."

King actually takes a step back, like he might try to run. "I'll try."

"No!" Cecily snaps at us. "There's no 'try' in this. Only doing."

Coop snickers again, and this time all three of us glare at him. "Alright, I can see where I'm not wanted. Have fun with your little project, *Mrs.* Yoda. You'll be lucky if they're both in one piece at the end of all this."

He wanders off, and though he was probably joking, there's a good chance I *won't* be making it to the other side in one piece if Cecily is truly going to make us go through the process of counseling, or whatever it is she plans to do. I'm likely to end with a heart split in two.

Chapter Fourteen

King

I KNEW IT WAS too much to hope, but I'm still irritated when I discover Cecily wasn't kidding about working around our schedules and finding time to push Georgie and me together. She left me alone that first day after talking to Vanderman, during which I reorganized the surf shop until it was late enough for me to go home and crash without talking to either Georgie or her friend, but I just finished up my last lesson today, and Cecily is standing in the surf shop doorway with a wicked gleam in her eyes.

Georgie is right behind her looking green.

"This place is darling!" Cecily says by way of greeting.

I ignore her and keep my focus on my wife. *My wife.* That's a phrase that's been on repeat for two days, and I'm not thrilled about it. I was starting to get used to the idea, but now it's like my brain needs it front and center at all times. "How was your day?" I ask Georgie.

She shrugs. "Pretty normal."

Cecily's gaze snaps back to her. "Excuse me?"

Georgie sighs. "I met with Beck today and talked about possible updates to the layout."

I try to hide the sharp pains that shoot through my chest at the thought of anything in that bakery changing, but I'm not sure I manage it. I know it needs some renovations, but I'm still worried I'm going to step inside one day and not recognize the place. I don't think Georgie's that heartless, but what do I know?

Maybe the sharp pain is a repeat of my worries from the other night at the pool hall. I don't think Beck would go for Georgie, but...

Clearing my throat, I busy myself with closing out the register. If only I had a valid reason to run away from this conversation, but I don't. "And?"

"He thinks we can make all the changes pretty quickly, though we'll have to do it in pieces so I can stay open while he works."

"That's great." At least it won't be a total overhaul, but now I'm imagining my friend wielding his contractor muscles while Georgie sits on the counter and watches him work, with a plate of warm chocolate chip cookies ready for him on her lap. I shudder. "Beck is good at what he does."

"Ahem." That's Cecily, and I already know what she's going to say next. "Do, Mr. Kingston. Remember, there's no trying when it comes to relationships."

I look up and meet Georgie's gaze again. Her almost-smile is enough to tell me she thinks this is as ridiculous as I do, but we don't really have a choice. Especially because we could have had to sit down with some snooty guy chosen by Mr. Vanderman, and that would have been a disaster. Cecily, at least, will have Georgie's best interest at heart, whatever that will mean in the end.

"I still don't love that you're making changes," I admit, knowing Cecily will likely keep pushing me until I speak my truths. And I'm not about to say anything about how I'm worried Georgie will fall for Beck, who is both friendly and generally considered attractive.

I don't know how Cecily knew I was going to be resistant to saying what I'm really feeling, but she seems to have me pinned down without even knowing me. I also don't know how Georgie is friends with this woman. Then again, Georgie has only ever been afraid to speak her mind once. I still have no idea why she ran from my proposal, and it's likely that I never will.

Georgie sighs. "I know you don't like it, but a lot of things need to be replaced. I'm sure even Bill would agree with me if he were here."

"Maybe, but he's not here to disagree either."

"I promise it will be worth it."

"Maybe," I agree again. But that won't change the fact that every renovation is going to be a step away from what's left of my family. One of these days I'll convince myself that a building doesn't equate to my uncle's memory, but I don't think that's going to be today.

"Here's what I think you two need," Cecily says, stepping into my line of sight so I have to look at her instead of Georgie. Ignoring my scowl, she reaches out a hand toward each of us. If she's expecting me to grab hold, she's got another thing coming. "I don't know enough about you, King, and I really want to see how well you work together so I know where we need to focus."

"What does that entail, exactly?" Georgie asks. Unlike me, she took Cecily's hand, but I think she's regretting that now that she's closer to Cecily's wild-eyed look. It's going to be a lot harder for her to escape, and if I have to leave her behind to get away from whatever Cecily is planning, I may not even look back.

Cecily wiggles her fingers at me for a few seconds and then gives up, instead lifting her hand to touch a finger to her lips. "That is an excellent question, Georgie. I have two options in mind for tonight. One King will probably hate, and the other I know you will."

"The first one," I say quickly, which surprises me as much as it seems to surprise them. I shrug as I try to figure out why I would choose something I'm not going to like. "I get the feeling we'll be doing both things at some point, so I might as well get the awful one over first."

"What if I want to use that argument?" Georgie asks.

"King beat you to it," Cecily says. "Therefore, we're heading to the bakery!"

Well, now I'm questioning my choice, and I have the sudden horrifying vision of being forced to hear about every single change Georgie wants to make and offer up my honest opinion. That is not going to end well for anyone unless I suddenly become a master of deception. There's no way I can look Georgie in the face and tell her flat-out that I will hate any change she wants to make, even if it's the truth.

This time, Cecily forcefully grabs my hand instead of offering hers to me, and she's pulling me out of the shop before I can protest.

I still try. "Wait! Can I lock up first?"

Cecily reluctantly lets me finish closing up the shack before she grabs hold again and pulls me to the boardwalk. The sun is starting to set, and Coral Berry is more crowded than it has been so far this season. It's like everyone and their dog—literally, there are a million dogs—decided to come to Willow Cove in the last couple of days and crowd the boardwalk. Before the meeting with Vanderman, I would have been glad for the cover of tourists so we won't be watched as closely by the locals, but now it means Georgie and I will be busier than ever.

"Why are we going to the bakery?" Georgie asks, a little breathless because Cecily is walking like a woman on a mission and dragging us with her. "I thought we were just going to sit around and talk for twenty minutes or something."

"Oh, but that's not going to work for you two. This counseling is going to require a special touch."

"I really don't like the sound of that," I say.

Cecily merely throws a grin at me.

Thankfully, the bakery is closed by this point so the place is blessedly quiet compared to the rest of the boardwalk. Bill always talked about maybe keeping the place open later in the day because inevitably several dozen tourists will try the door throughout the evening, but I'm glad we've kept to normal baking hours. They can go to Maggie's sweet shop down the way and try us again in the morning.

"Seriously, what are we doing here?" Georgie asks. "I already spent all day here, and while I love baking, I don't love it that much."

"Do you love it enough to walk King through how to make macarons?"

Georgie snorts. "Do you mean macaroons?"

"Excuse you, but which one of us has actually been to Paris? I mean macarons."

I have a vague idea what Cecily is talking about, and I'm pretty sure Georgie was making them before we went ring shopping. I also know Bill tried to make them a couple of times and ended up going on a tirade about French pastries when he couldn't get them to bake right.

"King can't make macarons," Georgie says, though she heads into the kitchen as if ready to face the challenge.

I follow her with a frown. "Why can't King make macarons?" I ask indignantly. She's probably right, but I don't like how little faith she has in me.

"Because they take a delicate hand, and you don't have those." As if she needs to demonstrate, she lifts my hand within view of my face. But then her eyes catch on the ring on my finger, and a spark of something comes to life in her eyes.

I tug my hand free as a fire sparks in my belly to match.

Turning to Cecily, who followed us into the kitchen, Georgie shakes her head. "I can show him, but that doesn't mean he's going to be able to do it."

"I didn't ask you to show him."

"You said—"

"I told you that you're going to walk him through it, which means you're not allowed to touch any of it."

I don't especially love that Georgie laughs out loud. "You've got to be kidding," she says.

"They can't be that hard," I throw in. "I've been able to make decent versions of everything in Bill's recipe book."

That's not necessarily true. There's a reason Meg started relegating me to cookie duty. But I like to think I can follow instructions as well as anyone and, knowing Georgie, she'll be incredibly particular with her directions.

Georgie's argument comes quickly. "Bill didn't make macarons."

"But you do," Cecily argues for me, raising an eyebrow at Georgie. "And if you want to convince this town and its questionable attorney that you are not a threat to their ecosystem, you need to prove that you trust this man enough to truly be his wife. AKA you have to trust him with something important to you. King is trusting you with his uncle's bakery, Georgie, and I don't think you realize how difficult this is for him."

Georgie's eyes meet mine, her eyebrows low, and while I would absolutely love to pretend Cecily is wrong, I can't. Maybe it's because it's coming from her friend, or maybe it hasn't been put in such clear terms before now, but Georgie seems to grasp my take on this for the first time.

"Okay," she says with a sigh. "King, I'm sorry. I know you're not getting a lot out of this deal."

"No, I'm not," I agree.

Cecily clears her throat. I don't know how she knows I'm holding back, but I'm getting the sense that she is very good at her job.

I roll my eyes. "But Kingston's was dying, and if you can save her, I have to let you do it. Even if I don't want you to change it."

"Georgie knows what she's doing," Cecily says and puts a hand on my arm.

I stare at it for a moment, but it's kind of nice being touched by someone who isn't flirting with me. That doesn't happen often. Okay, wow, I should really get out more. I sound pathetic.

"She's been dreaming up her own bakery for years," Cecily continues, "and you should have seen her talking to that Beck guy earlier. She loves this place, and she's going to make it shine."

With a warm smile toward her friend that I wish she reserved only for me, Georgie grabs a couple of aprons and hands one to me. "Okay, well, if we want to get these done before midnight, we'd better get started."

Cecily snatches the apron out of her hand before she can tie it. "You're not touching anything, Georgiana, so you're not going to need this. How about you take a seat?"

Georgie is clearly not happy about being forced into the office chair, but she doesn't argue. Cecily grabs another chair from the lobby for herself, and then she motions for us to begin.

"Okay," Georgie says with a bit of strain in her voice. "First, you're going to need to whip up some egg whites..."

Forty-five minutes later, I'm covered in powdered sugar and ready to storm out of the bakery in frustration, Georgie is going hoarse from shouting at me, and Cecily is having way too much fun for someone who, as far as I'm aware, is on our side. I'm starting to doubt that part.

"You're supposed to be tucking the kids in for bed, Kingston!" Georgie says. "Not drowning your enemies in a bathtub!"

"That analogy doesn't even make sense," I growl. I'm attempting to fold the almond flour mixture into the green-colored egg whites, but apparently I'm being too aggressive. If I was holding the spatula any lighter, I wouldn't be touching it at all.

Georgie lasted in her chair for about five minutes, and she's been hovering over me ever since. The only reason she hasn't taken the bowl out of my hands is because Cecily tied her hands behind her back, but that hasn't stopped her from leaning on my arm as if she might telepathically control my hands for me. "You're doing it all wrong," she complains.

"I know what 'fold' means," I argue. "Contrary to what you seem to believe, I'm not completely useless." Though, Georgie's doing a great job of making me feel that way. "I lived with Uncle Bill for almost a decade, so I did pick up a thing or two."

"Yeah, well, Bill wasn't exactly a trained pastry chef, was he?" As soon as the words are out of her mouth, Georgie winces. "I didn't mean... I'm sorry. I loved Bill. You know I did."

My own words come out rough but quiet. "You have a funny way of showing it."

She sighs. "I know. You just need to..." She nods toward the half-mixed bowl of batter in front of us. "If you don't mix it gently, you'll knock all the air out of the egg whites."

"Oh." I frown at the mixture. "I didn't realize that was the reason for all of this 'tucking into bed' nonsense."

Chuckling, Georgie nudges my arm, which I take as an invitation to keep mixing. "It was the best I could come up with. If I knew anything about surfing, I would have found a surf analogy."

"Did you ever go surfing with King over the summers?" Cecily asks.

"No," we both say together.

I tried so many times to convince her to at least try it, but Georgie's fear of the ocean is strong. I don't blame her, but it would have made those summers when we were young all that much better. I enjoyed doing the things she wanted to do, but surfing is in my soul. I would have loved to share that part of me with her.

"Hmm," Cecily says and jots something down on the iPad she pulled out soon after we started this macaron business. Apparently she really meant it when she said she would do her job right, and I'm terrified of what Vanderman might end up reading at the end of these two weeks. If tonight is any proof, Georgie and I are both a little too hard-headed to play nicely with each other.

Georgie clears her throat, pulling my attention back to the macaron batter. "A couple more times, and I think you'll be good. Through the middle and around the sides..."

I do as she tells me, though I honestly can't say with certainty that it's mixed all the way through. "This is ridiculously complicated for a little cookie."

"Macaronage is something every pastry chef hates at first, but once you get the hang of it, it's not that bad."

"When did you learn all this? You didn't go to school or anything."

Georgie smiles, and it seems like she's lost in memory. "I learned most things from Bill, and then I practiced other techniques during the rest of the year by watching videos online and reading recipe blogs. I got a job at a really good bakery not long after I met Cecily."

We both glance at Cecily, who grins back at us before jotting down some more notes. A cheery chime fills the space a second later, and she looks down at her phone. "It's Jet," she says, lifting the phone to her ear and slipping out into the lobby with her iPad tucked under her arm.

"Her husband," Georgie explains.

"Ah."

For a moment, she and I stand here and look at each other, like neither of us is sure what we should do now that we're no longer under the watchful gaze of our therapist. There's no question Cecily will be back at some point and expecting us to continue, but what do we do in the meantime?

"You'll need a piping bag next," Georgie says after clearing her throat. When I open a drawer to grab one, only to find it full of towels instead, she bites her lip. "Sorry. I moved them to that one over there. It helps my flow by having that stuff closer to where I usually do the piping work."

I ignore the flash of irritation that rushes through me. "Smart." I mean that, even if the word came out a little rough. I can't expect Georgie to operate exactly the same way Uncle Bill did, and swapping drawers isn't the same as erasing someone's memory.

With a piping bag in hand, I start loading up the batter and search for another topic of conversation. If I can keep her talking, she's less likely to judge the mess I'm making as I try to get all the batter into the bag. "What about that fancy boyfriend of yours?" I ask. I regret it instantly but keep going. "Did you learn anything from him?"

I'm not sure I want to know what prompts the blush on her cheeks.

"Baking-wise, he learned more things from me than the other way around. We met on the set of that competition I was in, and the only reason he got first place was because the final challenge was his specialty. He got lucky. Most of the stuff we sell in the *Home Baked* bakery are my recipes."

"So why is he the one who gets to keep the show and stuff now that you've split up?"

She huffs in frustration. "That is a good question, Kingston. His name is the one behind the company, so he made the argument that I have no claim, and I was too tired of his crap to fight it."

Now he *really* sounds like an idiot, and I think I might understand why she wants to own Kingston's instead of keeping it under my name. All things considered, she's been very calm about everything even though it hasn't been going exactly how she hoped. If it were me, I wouldn't be able to hide my frustration.

She looks down at the half-full bag in my hands and nods. "Ready to start piping? You're going to pipe in a circle, starting at the side and working your way to the center, and you'll want to make them about an inch and a half in diameter without ending with a point in the middle. I would demonstrate for you if I could." She shrugs her shoulders. "Do one, and I'll tell you if you're doing it right."

"How magnanimous of you."

"That's a fun word. Not exactly a surf term, so where'd you pick that one up? A little smaller."

I furrow my brow, as much in confusion as concentration as I do my best to pipe out the round cookies to her specifications. "You do know I went to college, don't you?"

"What?" She bumps into my arm so hard that she completely messes up the macaron I was piping. "Why didn't I know that?"

"Why didn't you ask?"

"I don't know. I guess since you're still working at the surf shack. You said you bought it when you were nineteen!"

I shrug, though it stings to think she wouldn't expect me to continue my education. I know I'm small-town, but I like to think I have a big life ahead of me. Or, I did before Uncle Bill passed away and made me the last Kingston. Now dreaming of more for my life seems pointless. "The shack is only open part of the year, and Pete still managed it for those first few years while I was going to Charleston Southern. I worked the shop in the afternoons."

"You still lived in Willow Cove?"

"It wasn't that long of a drive, and I did half my classes online. I thought about moving to Charleston for the last couple of years, but I liked being around Uncle Bill too much."

"What did you study?"

"Business." And I would really like to talk about something that isn't me. "You know people can have good vocabularies without getting a degree, right? You don't have a degree, so you should be offended by your own surprise that I would use a word like *magnanimous*."

Color floods her face, but she smiles a little, so she's not entirely embarrassed. She nods to the half-full tray in front of me. "Those aren't completely terrible."

"You're not completely terrible," I shoot back and then pipe a little circle of macaron batter onto her forehead.

She gasps, mouth gaping open. "I can't believe you just did that. Especially when I can't fight back!"

"We can't have that." I move in close, which both works to shut her mouth and gets me near enough to reach behind her. Working slowly, I tug loose the apron strings that have held her hands captive behind her back. I'm taking my time both so I can prepare for her counterstrike and because I've got a noseful of her intoxicating scent. I could stand here all night. "Never let it be said that I don't fight fair," I whisper.

When my fingers brush against Georgie's hand, she curls her fingers around mine for a brief moment. A gesture of gratitude for freeing her, maybe? Regardless, her touch is as electric as it has been since her return, and I can't help but close my eyes as I take another deep breath of the smell of her shampoo.

When I open my eyes again, I'm overcome by how beautiful she is. I've always thought so, but I must have forgotten how it felt to gaze into those green eyes of hers and see everything. All of her fears and hopes. There were times when I thought I could hear her thoughts just by looking at her, and I've either lost the skill or she's saying there's a chance she might stay. *Please stay.*

Georgie grabs the piping bag from my other hand and squeezes it in my direction. The green goop oozes out too slowly and plops onto the floor between our feet. We stare at it for a moment, neither of us saying a word, and then I crack, snorting a chuckle that quickly turns into a full-blown laugh when Georgie starts giggling.

We both have the idea at the same time, our hands flying to the remainder of the batter in the bowl. I'm faster by only a second and manage to get a good slather across Georgie's face before she's stuffing a handful of slimy paste down my shirt. Gasping from the cold of it, I instinctively wrap my arms around her to hold her captive, but her messy hand is still free and ends up in my hair.

"That's it." Ignoring the shiver of pleasure that runs through me from her touch, I duck down and throw her over my shoulder. "You're getting blasted."

Georgie screams as I head for the industrial sink and the spray nozzle that has always felt akin to a fire hydrant with the way it gushes at high speed. "No! Royal! I give up! You win."

I'm tempted to keep going, but I stop and set her back on her feet because she has never conceded before. But I keep hold of her in case I need to follow through with my threat when she inevitably tries to pull a fast one on me. Still, now that I have a good view of her face again, I can't hold back my laugh. "You're a mess."

She smacks my chest half-heartedly, leaving her hand resting there. "I can't believe you did that! And you can't claim that I started it this time."

No, I can't, but I'm not finding the will to apologize. Not with the way she's grinning at me right now. "You mean a faceful of macaron mess wasn't part of your directions?" Using the heel of my hand, I brush some of the batter from her cheek, but it's going to take a lot more than that to get her clean.

Despite the pale green mixture all over her skin, her eyes seem to glow beneath the kitchen lights, the most vivid green I've ever seen. I don't know if anything will ever compare to her eyes. Windows to her incredible soul. "You know me better than that, Royal," she says, leaning closer.

My heart starts pounding beneath her fingers, pushing me forward until my nose brushes hers. "Yeah, I do." *Please stay.*

I can almost taste her, but a small voice in the back of my head reminds me there is no one we need to convince right now. If I kiss her now, it's simply because I want to. And that will make this all so much messier. Maybe she's thinking the same thing, or maybe my hesitation has communicated something else to her, but it's Georgie who pulls away first.

"Um," she says, taking a step back, "we need to let those sit for at least half an hour before we bake them. Maybe longer. But I should probably..."

Her eyes focus on something behind me, and I turn to see Cecily sitting on the counter nearest the door to the lobby. I have no idea how long she's been there or how much of our interaction she saw, but she's writing furiously on her iPad and grinning in a way that sends a chill down my spine. I don't want to know what she thinks she's learned tonight.

"You should go to bed," I reluctantly tell Georgie. "I can clean up here."

Maybe I imagine it, but she seems disappointed. "Are you sure? I can—"

"I've got this. You take care of you." *Stay.*

"Okay." She takes a step back and smiles. "Goodnight, Royal."

That's not the first time she called me that tonight, and for some reason the name doesn't bother me. Maybe it's because right now she feels more like the old Georgie, and in turn I feel more like myself for the first time in a long time.

I watch her leave arm in arm with Cecily, and when I run a hand through my hair and find it full of macaron batter, I can't help but smile.

Chapter Fifteen

Georgie

FOR THE NEXT FEW days, Cecily says she has work to do and camps out in her hotel room, only joining me for lunch and dinner each day. She keeps our conversation to anything that *isn't* the happenings in Willow Cove or my marriage, which is becoming increasingly more frustrating because she won't say a word about what she's planning to tell Mr. Vanderman.

The only comment she *has* made so far was the day after the macaron situation, after I found a little plastic baggie filled with poorly assembled macarons and tied with a ribbon. King baked the cookies, which didn't rise properly, and sandwiched a few of them with light green frosting that was incredibly lumpy but properly proportioned. They weren't much to look at, but they tasted good, and the fact that he finished the task without direction from me seemed to please Cecily.

"How sweet of your husband," she said.

That has been the only mention of King in *days*, and I am terrified about what's coming next from her.

I've seen King a couple of times, mostly when he's on his way in to the surf shack. He tries to stop by the bakery whenever Mrs. Vanderman is in the lobby, and though we've avoided any kissing, like there's an unspoken agreement between us to forgo that necessity if we can, I've started getting used to my morning hugs from Royal Kingston.

Hugs from that man are life-giving.

I've also fallen into the habit of calling him Royal again. He hasn't corrected me, so either he's giving in because he thinks it's stubbornness fueling the change and is tired of fighting me, or he is starting to like his name. I don't remember him ever letting anyone call him by his first name except me, and the allowance now has set a fire in my belly.

When it comes to this version of King, I think every step he allows me in his direction is a big thing. And I find myself wanting to take whatever steps I can.

"So you don't have to answer this if you don't want to," Emily says as she wipes down the front counter. For the first time in days, we don't have any customers, and both of us are enjoying the quiet. At least, I was until Emily started her inquiry. "But how did you and King meet?"

Though I would like to keep reading this blog about which country has the best butter for baking, I can tell Emily has been wanting to ask this question for a long time. Probably since the day I showed up in Willow Cove.

I give her a smile and put my phone in my pocket. "It was actually here in the bakery when we were twelve."

She gasps, eyes going comically wide. "Really?"

"Yep. It's probably hard to imagine, but King was all limbs back then." I look at the wall of pictures behind me, hunting for one of my favorites. "Ah! Here he is. He's probably fourteen or so in this one."

The picture is one of Bill and King, both clutching surf boards and looking bedraggled. Like I told Emily, King is tall and gangly in his wetsuit, though it's easy to tell that he's starting to fill out with surfing muscles. His dark hair flops in his eyes, but his smile makes it clear he couldn't be happier with his current situation.

Emily hurries over to check out the picture. "Oh my gosh, he's so cute! I've never really looked at these pictures before." She starts examining them all, taking in the documentation of Bill's bakery from its humble beginnings up until what I'm guessing isn't long before he died.

I look a little more closely as well, surprised to see how many pictures of King are on this wall. There's a photo of eighteen-year-old King in a graduation gown, King cutting a ribbon in front of the newly renovated surf shack, King on the campus of Charleston Southern University. As they go along, the pictures are less and less about the bakery and more about the Kingston family, even if that family was just the two of them.

The picture with the surfboards was probably taken right before King's mom died and Bill took him in. Bill was never annoyed that he had to take care of his nephew, and sometimes I was pretty sure he was grateful to have someone with him. Bill and I spent a lot of time together over the summers, and he was always so proud of the person King was becoming. He liked to say whoever earned King's love would be a lucky person indeed, and he always had a mischievous glint in his eye when he did.

I don't think I was lying when I told Mr. Vanderman that Bill wanted King and me to get together.

"Why did you guys take so long to get married?" Emily asks, still checking out the photos.

My answer comes more easily than I expect it to. "Because I was scared."

"Scared of King?"

"Scared of missing out on the life I thought I was supposed to live."

Emily giggles a little and returns to cleaning the countertop. "At least you figured out it doesn't get better than being with King!"

Did I figure that out? A week ago, I would have said no, but every time he leaves the bakery with a warm smile, a part of me aches for him to stay. I've been more relaxed over the last week than I've been in years, and as much as I don't want to admit it out loud, Willow Cove is starting to feel like home.

Maybe my dreams were all wrong. What if it wasn't control I craved but knowing I would be okay even when things go wrong? I know I can find that safety with King because it has always been there. Since the day I met him. He's the steadiest person I've ever known. What if I...

The bell above the door jingles, and excitement rushes through me when Cecily steps inside.

"Finally!" The word rushes out of me.

My friend lifts an eyebrow. "Finally?"

"I was starting to think you'd never show up."

"You miss me that much?"

"Yes?"

Cecily's grin turns devilish. "Why did that sound like a question, Georgie?"

It wasn't supposed to be, and I don't know why my heart rate has kicked up a notch. "It wasn't a question! I'm always glad to see you, Cece."

"You're glad to see me because it means you get to see King."

Absolutely. "Do I? I thought you were here to see me."

"I am here to save your marriage." She grabs my hand and starts dragging me to the door. "Emily, Meg and Rebecca will be here soon!"

While I'm glad Cecily made sure my teenage employee won't be on her own, I get caught up on the first thing she said, nearly tripping over the doorway on the way out. "You mean *solidify* my marriage, right?" This marriage won't be lasting long enough for it to ever need saving.

My stomach twists.

In true Cecily fashion, she doesn't say a word until we reach the surf shop. Though King is in the middle of a conversation with a girl who looks like she was born to surf—long, strong legs, glowing bronze skin, silky blonde hair running down her back in a thick braid—Cecily makes an announcement to the whole shop in her loudest voice. "Kingston, your next lesson is here!" Then she shoves me forward.

I squeak at the same time King's eyes go wide. "What?" I gasp.

King swallows. "I thought *you* wanted to learn, Cecily."

"Why would I want to learn how to surf? The ocean is terrifying."

"Something we agree on!" I complain.

Folding his arms, King glances at the girl next to him and then to the open doors, like he's considering running away. He doesn't need to worry; it's not like I'm ever going to get on a surfboard, no matter what Cecily says. "Lacey," he says to the girl, "maybe you can take this one?"

Lacey eyes me with a raised eyebrow. "Don't you want to teach your wife, King?"

"That would be a bad idea," he says at the same time I say, "I don't want to learn."

"Too bad," Cecily says behind me. "This is your next counseling session, and Mr. Vanderman was curious about how things are going and wanted to watch this one."

King swears under his breath. I'm starting to wonder why he's so opposed to this. He's not the one who will be fearing for his life.

I need to find a way out of this. "I don't have a swim—"

Cecily holds a polka-dotted piece of fabric in front of my face. "And yes, it's in your size."

"It's also in two pieces," I point out. I'm all for women expressing themselves with fun swimwear, but this baker's body prefers to be a little more covered. "I have one at home. I can go—"

"Run and hide?" Cecily stuffs the suit into my hands and pushes me toward the changing room on the left side of the shop. "It'll just be you and your husband out on the water, Georgie. You'll be fine."

"My husband and Mr. Vanderman, apparently."

"Like the old man's going to be able to see you from the shore."

"But—"

"Georgie," King says, cutting through our argument. "You can pick anything on the rack. It's fine."

Releasing a breath of relief, I scurry to the rack of swimsuits before Cecily can keep trying to push the bikini. While I'm sure King would have appreciated seeing me in something more revealing, which was likely Cecily's reasoning, I can't help but love how easily he offered a better option. I'm not especially self-conscious—I love butter and sugar too much to worry about my figure—but I'm going to need to be as comfortable as possible for this. Grabbing the first suit that I find in my size, I hop into the changing room and do my best to ignore the fact that I'm going to have to go out into the ocean to save my bakery.

That logic seems questionable, but nothing about this whole thing has made a lot of sense.

As I change, I listen intently to the conversation happening outside the door, since King and Cecily aren't trying to keep their voices down.

"If she doesn't want to learn, I'm not taking her out there," King says. "No matter if Vanderman is watching."

"You agreed to make macarons," is Cecily's argument, which isn't the same at all. "So the least she can do is—"

"Almond flour isn't the ocean, Cecily. I never pushed Georgie to go surfing because the last thing I want to do is put her in danger."

I press a hand to the changing room door as warmth spreads through me. He's a good man and always has been. I don't know if I could ever find a better man than him.

"You're not going to let her get hurt," Cecily says. "I know you won't. I also know how Georgie can be, and while most of the time it's easier to let her steamroll and blaze her own trail, she needs to learn that she can't go through life alone. Sometimes she needs to relinquish her control and trust that someone else can lead the way."

King doesn't have a reply to that, which settles like a rock in my stomach. I know I'm headstrong, but... His words from our wedding day flicker into my memory. *I can't get caught up in your orbit just for you to leave me drifting again.* That was how my relationship was with Lane. He was always making the decisions and pulling me along with him, ignoring my ideas but taking credit for them when he inevitably presented them as his own. His way was the only way.

I wouldn't wish a relationship like that on anyone.

It's that thought that spurs me forward with a new determination. Tugging on the suit, which is one of those sport-types that are meant for function rather than fashion, I hurry back out to the lobby and breathlessly announce, "I want to try it! At least once."

King gapes at me. It's like he didn't in a million years think I would agree, which only makes my guilt worse. Then his eyes slip down over my body, and the guilt is quickly replaced with heat as his expression morphs into thinly veiled desire. Apparently I *don't* need a bikini to prove my husband is attracted to me.

"There, you see?" Cecily says, but even she seems surprised that I agreed. Maybe she hadn't intended for us to go surfing at all and simply thought the argument would count as counseling. "I'll, uh, go see if Mr. Vanderman has arrived yet." She wanders out almost in a daze.

"I've got the shop covered," Lacey says, and I'm pretty sure she's trying not to laugh. Whether she's laughing at me or something else, I can't bring myself to care as long as King keeps looking at me with that fire blazing in his eyes. I would let him look at me like this forever.

It takes several seconds before King finally moves, heading for the row of surfboards with a rigidness to his posture that wasn't there before I put on the swimsuit. Maybe I'm not lithe and limber, but these bread-kneading biceps are clearly doing it for the man I married, and I'm going to take a lot of pride in that fact.

For the next hour, King seems to do his best to pretend I'm just another student, though I notice he rarely looks at me as he goes through his process. When he does look, he tends to lose his train of thought, so I get it. He walks me through how to stand up and balance while still on the sand, and he describes the general mechanics of catching a wave's momentum. He asks me multiple times if I'm sure about going out on the water. I'm not, but I also know that if he's out there with me, I'll be okay.

I want him to know that I care about the things he cares about, even if they scare me.

"Watch this one," he says, pointing to a surfer who starts paddling to catch the wave. "She's going to paddle until the wave starts moving her faster than she's going on her own, and then..."

The woman jumps to her feet and turns her board so it goes in the opposite direction of where the wave is curling over.

"I'm guessing I'll need to pay attention to the way the wave breaks," I say, gesturing vaguely at the wave as it crashes and dissipates. The movement brings me close enough to King that our arms touch, and a thrill runs through me when he doesn't pull away. It's not like I haven't touched this man—we've kissed twice since getting married and shared plenty of hugs—but something about today is different.

I'm telling myself that it's because we're being watched by the sunscreen-soaked attorney under the giant umbrella, but I'm pretty sure that's a lie.

No, I *know* it's a lie. I desperately wanted to kiss King when we were at the bakery the other night, and not because I wanted to make a point. Because I *wanted* to. Yesterday, when an adorable old couple came into the bakery and went on and on about how they have been coming to Kingston's every summer for the last eight years since discovering it, I instantly wanted to tell King about them so we could smile about it together. When I woke up this morning, I found Prince Harry splashing in the pool. He isn't likely to drown now that the water level is lower, but I figured it would be good to get him back in his pen. So I hunted down a rope and spent almost an hour guiding him to the stairs and tugging him up and out because I didn't want to wake King. He'd gotten home later than normal and looked tired as he walked around the house without a shirt on before going to bed.

And yeah, I was spying on him from the pool house instead of going to sleep, but I couldn't help it.

Basically, every moment of my day has started to include King in it, whether he's present or not. I'm getting addicted to this man, and I'm not sure it's a habit I want to kick. Standing on a beach in the last few hours of daylight, watching the crash of waves and listening to the sounds of happy vacationers, I'm starting to realize that I am still very much in love with the man next to me.

Not sure I ever really stopped loving him.

"Well, what do you think?" King says, looking at me for the first time in several minutes. "Want to try hitting a wave before it gets too late?"

"You'll be with me?" I hate that my voice shakes on that question, but the ocean is still just as terrifying as it always has been.

King grabs hold of my hand and squeezes it. "Always, Shortcake."

Oh goodness, he hasn't called me that in years, and I can't help but giggle. It's a callback to when we first met and he came barreling into the bakery right as I was about to eat a strawberry cupcake. He thought it was hilarious and brought it up the next time we met, calling me Strawberry Shortcake even though that is a different dessert entirely. He quickly shortened it to Shortcake and claimed it was because I wasn't very tall—I'm still not—but we both knew the day we met was an exceptionally good day that had impressed upon both of us. I always made sure to tell him I hated the nickname, knowing that would make him use it more often.

"I can't believe you remember that," I say, still grinning.

King chuckles. "I can't believe you didn't punch me for using it."

"*I* can't believe you've been letting me call you Royal."

He actually grins at that, his eyes dancing in the golden light of the afternoon. "I can't believe you think I would hate anything you call me."

We definitely need to get in the water because I am about to spontaneously combust from the way he's looking at me right now. I don't know what changed between our macaron adventure and now, but this man isn't holding back.

I grab my surfboard, which is comfortably shorter than his and made of a hard foam instead of whatever his is made out of. "You really gave me the kiddie board, didn't you?"

He laughs. "A beginner's board, Georgie. This one is less likely to knock you out if you fall wrong."

"Wait, there's a wrong way to fall?"

"Come along, Shortcake. We don't have all day." With a light jog, he rushes into the water and hops onto his board, gliding effortlessly out into the deeper water.

I'm far less graceful but somehow manage to join him. Getting in the water is easy; paddling deeper is harder. But King lets me take my time, filling the space between us with more tips and tricks as if he knows that listening to him talk is the best distraction from the rapidly dropping ocean floor beneath me. I keep my eyes on his face. On his kind eyes and warm smile. I tell myself over and over again that I trust this man more than I trust anyone, and I want to show him as much.

By the time he thinks I'm ready to actually try to catch a wave, I'm shaking in my metaphorical boots but doing everything I can to hide it. I like to think I'm tough and adventurous, but this is so far beyond my capabilities and know-how.

Still, being out here and seeing up close King in his element is helping me see another side to him, which is crazy considering I've always known he loves surfing. I've always loved watching him from the shore. But I didn't know to what extent he loses all his inhibitions out here and looks entirely relaxed, and I want him to be this happy all the time.

He's lost so much in his life, and I wish I had been brave enough to understand how much I hurt him when he lost me too. Will he survive when I leave again?

A pit forms in my belly at the thought of leaving this place. It feels a lot like the feeling I would get at the end of the summer when I was young, not yet ready to go back home.

"Watch me ride this next wave," King says, oblivious to my fears. "Pay attention to the movement of the water now that you're up close."

It's definitely different now that I'm in deeper water, and I watch not only King, who is exceptional, but the few other surfers who are out here with us as well. Theoretically I can mimic what they're all doing, but I don't have a lot of faith in my actual ability. Piping too-cold frosting isn't the same level of skill as riding a wave that has the power to shove me deep under the water if I'm not careful. I can swim, but...the ocean is a beast unto itself.

Returning to my side, King reaches over and grabs my trembling hand. "No one will think less of you if you decide to go back to shore," he says gently. "Just having you out on the water with me has made me happier than I can say."

"It was always so easy to make you happy," I murmur.

He actually blushes, though he ducks his head to hide it. "Not so much lately. Ever since Uncle Bill died, I think there's been a shadow hanging over me that won't go away. I don't know if it ever will."

I squeeze his fingers. "Maybe if we ride a wave together you can have a little sunshine."

I don't even know if we can share these waves, which aren't exactly large, but that doesn't stop a grin from spreading across his face. "Can't hurt to try."

It hurts a lot, in fact.

On my first attempt to pop up and get to my feet on a wave, the nose of the board takes a dive and sends me tumbling face first into the whitewater. Something hits my head hard, and the next thing I know I'm on the shore with King's frantic face looming over me as I choke on the water in my lungs.

"Georgie!" he says, the word a little garbled. "Can you hear me?"

I cough and then grimace when everything hurts, from my lungs to my head. I swallow, my tongue tasting salt. "What happened?"

He exhales with relief and then pushes my hair out of my face. "You scared the crap out of me," he breathes. "I think the board hit you in the head when you wiped out, and then you didn't come up."

I don't remember any of that, but maybe that's a good thing. "Was it the most pathetic crash you've ever seen?"

He chuckles, though the worry hasn't left his eyes. "Nah. But maybe don't try surfing again, okay?"

"Deal."

"How's your head?"

It's throbbing, but everything is already becoming sharper, including my realization that King is practically lying on top of me in the wet sand. His body is warm, his skin smooth against mine, and I don't want him to move. Even if I feel a bit like Prince Eric after Ariel—King, in this case—rescues him from the storm. I highly doubt King will start singing to me, though.

"I think I'll live," I say slowly, "but I might need to take the morning off tomorrow."

Nodding, King runs his fingers through my bedraggled curls. His eyes keep roving over me, like he can't quite believe that I'm okay. "I'll text Meg."

"She might not listen."

"I'll pay her extra."

"You don't have to worry about the bakery anymore, Royal."

He smiles softly, and his thumb brushes across my cheekbone. "I know. But I'm worried about you."

I don't deserve that. I don't deserve the warm concern in his eyes, or the gentle touch of his fingers, or the pleasure of lying this close to him, in the sand or otherwise. He deserves someone who will stick around, and that's not me.

What's making you leave?

The voice that asks that question sounds an awful lot like Cecily. But it also sounds like myself. I used to have a ready answer, but now I'm coming up blank. I certainly don't want to leave right now.

"Do you think you can sit up?" King asks. "Cecily went to grab your clothes and a towel, but I think we should probably get you into bed after a crash like that."

I'm exhausted, and my bed is calling to me like a siren song I can't resist. I want nothing more than to sleep for days.

Except, as King helps me to my feet and then presses me up against his side in a sturdy embrace that shuts out the world, I think that statement might be wrong.

I think I might want him more.

Chapter Sixteen

King

THE STORM ROLLS IN around ten, wild and angry. Weather like this isn't un-common in South Carolina, but there's something about tonight that makes it impossible to sleep. It's the heavy rain pounding against the roof. It's wondering what went through Vanderman's head when he watched me nearly have to give my wife mouth-to-mouth because she got forced into surfing. It's reliving that moment when Georgie wiped out and got caught in a washing machine, tossed about in the waves until I could finally reach her.

I know it was a matter of chance that her crash was that bad, but the whole thing terrified me. I could have lost her today, and in that fleeting moment when I thought maybe I had, after I dragged her to shore and waited for her to breathe, I came to a stark realization:

I can't let Georgie leave again.

That fiercely independent woman has always made me want to be more, do more, say more because she is unafraid of giving herself the life she wants. She's the reason I bought the surf shop instead of being content to simply work there. She's the reason I got a business degree in the hopes of expanding the shop or maybe even investing in something that's open year-round. I've been trying to keep up with her since the day I met her, and being in her orbit has only ever made my life better. Who cares if I'm always following her instead of the other way around?

If I have to follow her to the other side of the world, I'll do it.

Thunder rumbles across the sky, and I roll over to my other side, wondering how the pool house is holding up in the rain. I didn't see any signs of water damage, so the roof should be good, but it's also been a while since we had rain this heavy.

"If there's a problem, she'll come inside," I tell myself and roll over again, trying to get comfortable. I'm exhausted after pulling Georgie out of the water, and I really need to get some sleep.

After another hour of tossing and turning, I decide I should go out and double check that she's sound asleep. I don't think she got a concussion, but she's going to need some good rest after a wipe out like that. Plus, Georgie is stubborn enough that she might not come to me if something is going wrong, so I should make sure she's fine.

I curse when I get to the back door and see the light on in the pool house. It's nearly midnight, and that light wasn't on when the storm first broke.

Rushing across the yard, I flinch against the sharp raindrops pelting me and then knock on Georgie's door, keeping the sound light in case for some reason she's fallen asleep with the light on. When she doesn't answer, I nudge the door open and poke my head inside.

I swear again at the sight of Georgie curled up in a ball on the far corner of the bed while water steadily drips into a bowl in the middle of the mattress.

"Georgie!"

She grimaces and peeks one eye open. "Royal?"

That ceiling is going to need patching, but not tonight. "Why didn't you come to the house?"

She shrugs one shoulder and curls up even tighter. "You don't want—"

"I don't want you to be miserable. Come inside."

I'm not actually going to give her a choice in the matter, but I hold my hand out to her and hope she grabs it so I don't have to pick her up and carry her to the house against her will. Thankfully, she accepts my offered fingers and slowly clambers to her feet. She's a little unsteady, and I'm pretty sure she's shivering, but she manages to climb off the bed and into my arms.

I hold her as tightly as I dare, worried that I might hurt her or scare her off if I don't tread lightly. "I'm sorry," I say into her hair.

She tucks herself into my hold, her arms folded up between us. "You can do a lot of things, Royal Kingston," she says, "but I'm pretty sure you can't control the weather."

"I'm sorry for what happened on the water today."

"I'm not. But even if I am, I'm blaming Cecily. "

I chuckle. "I thought *you* were a steamroller, but she might be worse."

"She's so much worse," Georgie agrees. "I, at least, don't force other people along with me. I'm perfectly happy to go forward on my own."

I hope that isn't true. Surely life is better with someone else along for the ride, right? I'm too scared to ask. The last time I asked to be a part of her future, she ran away. I won't make that same mistake twice.

"Ready to go inside?" I ask instead. "I guarantee it'll be warmer and drier."

She nods against my chest, and together we dash through the rain to the house. Georgie immediately moves toward the front room and the couch, but I grab her hand to stop her.

"I'm not letting you sleep on that monstrosity," I say when she turns a questioning look toward me.

Biting her lip, she looks toward my bedroom and sends a jolt of electricity through me. "I'm not kicking you out of your bed."

"I know."

Color rises up her face, matching the heat building inside me. "King..."

I know exactly where her thoughts are going—mine are already there—but I shake my head. She nearly drowned today, and I'm still grappling with the ramifications of my ever-growing feelings for her. Neither of us is ready for something we can't take back. Right now, our marriage is only temporary. Until that changes...

"We're both adults," I tell her. "We can share a bed without it getting..." *Weird* is probably the wrong word, and *heated* is too close to the truth.

A smile ticks up Georgie's lips. "Intimate?" she suggests.

I growl. "That is so much worse than what I came up with."

She takes a step closer, then another, and I can't help but track her movement with the concentration of a stalking lion. "You should probably know that I have a tendency to sleepwalk."

I force my gaze to remain fixed on her face, though it isn't helping that she's in those short shorts again. Why couldn't she have worn one of those oversized nightgowns that old ladies wear? Then again, Georgie would probably be just as alluring no matter what she wears.

I clear my throat, once again forcing my traitorous eyes up to her face. "I didn't know that about you."

"Yeah, well, you've never slept with me before."

I take a step back to keep a certain level of space between us. "Are you likely to sleepwalk tonight?" I ask. Maybe bunking on the couch will be a better idea than sharing the bed with her, at least until we can have a thorough conversation about this marriage of ours and where it's going. I don't want to discover the kinds of things she might do in semi-consciousness. Not with the way she's looking at me right now.

Those expressive eyes of hers are setting a fire in my belly that's not going to be extinguished anytime soon.

Georgie shrugs, stepping forward until my back hits the wall, and then she grins. I desperately want her to touch me, but she doesn't. I feel her eyes, though. They trace my face and work their way down. "It's impossible to know if I'll sleepwalk or not. The last time, I ended up outside and was nearly eaten by a llama." A shiver runs through her, and I don't think it's because of Prince Harry.

Sighing, I pull her into my arms again and close my eyes as I memorize how it feels to hold her. It could be the only time I get the chance; I can't let myself hope too fully that we can make this work. We tried once, and she ran away.

The difference this time is I fully plan to follow her if she does that again. No cowardice this time around.

"We'll have to risk it," I tell her. "I need to know you're safe and warm tonight." *Every night. For the rest of our lives. Stay.*

Once I get her settled in my bed with all the blankets she could possibly need, I stretch out beside her and let my breath out in a steady stream, forcing myself to relax. I'm probably not going to get any sleep tonight, knowing she's there breathing next to me, but I don't care. As long as she's safe.

"Royal?"

I smile at the sound of my name. "Yeah?"

"Thanks for rescuing me today."

A replay of her wipeout flashes through my mind again, and I search for her fingers so I can make sure she's really here. Really safe. Her hand is cool against mine, and I hold it tight, trying to warm her fingers. "I'm sorry I had to. I shouldn't have let you—"

"I'm glad I did. I've always wondered what it's like out on the water with you. You..." She takes a deep breath, letting it out slowly. "You were born for the ocean. You looked so happy out there."

"I was happy," I admit. "Up until I thought you might drown."

"How about we agree that I'm better on dry ground?"

"Happily." Especially if she stays within sight. It's too dark to see her now, but I look at her anyway, trying to imagine the way her curls spill onto the pillow. I think she usually pulls her hair up at night, but tonight she left it down. Her curls were damp and frizzy from the rain, but she is beautiful. I don't have to see her to know that.

As a knot forms in my stomach, I change the topic of conversation to one that is far more dangerous than Georgie's understandable fear of the ocean. "How long do you think it will take to do the renovations on the bakery?"

She shifts, and I'm pretty sure she rolls over to face me. As long as she keeps holding my hand, I'll be happy. "It depends on how many of them I have Beck do."

"All of them." I probably say that too quickly, but I mean it. "You should make the bakery yours, Georgie."

I could be wrong, but I'm pretty sure she inches closer. "But what about you? What about Bill's legacy? I don't want to take him from you by changing everything you have left of him."

Lifting her hand up between us, I press my lips to her fingers. One by one. "Uncle Bill's legacy is you, Georgie. He always wanted you to have the bakery, and he wouldn't have expected you to be exactly like him. I know you'll honor him, no matter how you change things."

Georgie's other hand finds my cheek, scraping against the scruff and leaving a trail of warmth behind. I've missed this. I've missed *her*. The last two months have been the loneliest of my life, but with Georgie next to me, I don't feel like I'll ever be on my own again. I can't help but cling to that hope as tightly as I cling to her hand.

"I'm pretty sure his legacy is you, Royal," she says into the darkness. "He was so proud of you."

She can't know that, but her words settle warm and solid inside me anyway.

"I miss him," I admit. It's the first time I've said those words out loud, and they come out of me raw and rough. "It shouldn't have been harder to lose him than it was my parents, but it feels so much worse." And what kind of son does that make me, missing him more than I miss my own father?

"Hey." Georgie scoots closer, now pressing her whole palm to my cheek. "You were only eight when your dad died. And I *know* you were sad when you lost your mom. Some of your emails were heartbreaking, and I wanted so badly to be here with you."

Maybe that's the difference. When my mom died, I had Georgie to get me through it.

I shift forward until I can press my forehead to hers and breathe in her amazing scent, though it's mixed with the smell of rain, the ocean, and something that oddly reminds me of Prince Harry.

"I'm glad you're here with me now," I tell her. "You always make me feel stronger than I am."

That makes her laugh softly. "That's just ridiculous. I probably make you feel like you can't do anything because I'm too busy trying to do it myself."

"No." I touch a kiss to the tip of her nose. "I like following in your wake. You know what you want, and you don't let anyone tell you that you can't have it. It's inspiring. Everyone should want to be like you."

"Tell that to my ex. He hated following my lead."

"He's an idiot." I press my lips to hers because I can't help myself anymore. She tastes familiar, and it still feels like no time passed between our lives before and now. Her kiss is warm, exhilarating, invigorating. Everything I remember and so much better.

But Georgie responds more eagerly than I expect, and it takes everything in me to push her away.

"Oh, come on," she complains, trying to fight her way back to my mouth.

I chuckle. "Today was a big day, and you need to sleep."

"What if I want to—"

"*Georgie.*" I push my hand into her hair and groan. "I want to, believe me, but we should talk first. And not tonight." I hope she doesn't argue because my resolve is hanging by a thread. The most beautiful woman I've ever known is in my bed with me, trying to get closer, and I'm telling her to go to sleep. That probably makes me the biggest idiot in the world.

Sighing, she tugs her hand free from mine and twists around to face the other direction, which feels kind of petty. But then she cuddles up close, pressing herself flush against my body. "I don't understand you sometimes, Kingston," she mutters, but there's clear contentment in her voice as she settles into me.

I chuckle and wrap my arms around her, holding her close. I still might not sleep tonight, but I get to hold my wife as a storm rages around us, and that's more than I could ever need.

Chapter Seventeen

Georgie

I DON'T REMEMBER THE last time I slept long enough to be woken by sunlight streaming in through a window, and I can't decide if I love it or hate it. It's so bright, and I feel like I should be halfway through my day already instead of just opening my eyes. I *do* love waking up in King's arms, which is going to be a problem if he's not okay with this arrangement turning into an every night kind of thing.

He's still asleep behind me, his breaths coming in slow and deep. I wish I could see his face, but I'm not about to move and risk waking him up. I hope he looks happy and at peace. He seems like the kind of guy who worries about things even when asleep, and I hope last night eased some of his tension in the same way surfing does.

Granted, I would have loved to ease his tension another way last night, but I think he was right to set some boundaries.

We went into this marriage with one goal in mind, but I think that goal has changed for both of us. It would be smart to figure out exactly what that means before we take a step in any direction.

King's phone buzzes on the end table, either with a call or an alarm, and he starts to move as he wakes to the sound. His arms tighten around me, pulling me closer, and he starts nuzzling his nose into my neck with no sign of letting go. I could *definitely* get used to waking up like this.

"Five more hours," he moans softly.

"Do you mean minutes?" I ask with a laugh.

"I said what I said."

The phone stops vibrating, but a second later it starts up again.

He groans.

"Maybe it's something important," I say, tensing up a little when I think about my phone all the way out in the pool house. "Maybe you should check, just in case."

Sighing, he pulls himself free and rolls over to pick up the phone. "It's Emily," he says with another groan. "Is it bad that I want to make Meg handle whatever is happening?"

As a ribbon of unease threads through my gut, I snatch the phone out of his hand and answer it. "Emily? What's wrong?"

"Oh good, you're alive! I got worried when you didn't answer your phone because you always answer your phone but King tends to accidentally leave his at home sometimes so I wasn't sure if—"

"Emily!"

"Right. Um, someone is here at the bakery, and he says he won't go away until he talks to you."

I flip the phone to speaker even though King is close enough that he can probably hear everything she's saying anyway. "Who is he?"

"He won't say, but there's a guy with a camera here with him."

I sigh. That could be good or bad, but it sounds like I need to head to the bakery either way. More than likely it's related to *Home Baked*, whether it's someone from the show itself or a reporter who somehow figured out where I disappeared to.

"I'll be there soon, Emily. Thanks for letting me know." I hang up and then exhale all at once, flopping my arm back onto the bed while still hanging on to King's phone. "Is it bad that the only reason I think I should go to the bakery is because I don't want to leave whatever it is up to Meg? I still worry she's going to try sabotage at some point."

When King doesn't answer, I turn my head to look at him and find him gazing at me with hungry eyes. Apparently his reservations of last night aren't nearly as strong as they were before. His expression is enough to catch the sheets on fire.

I can't stop the smile that curls up my lips. I'm very much enjoying that look in his eyes, but I'm also enjoying the sight of his muscled body limned in soft sunlight as he lies stretched out beside me. "You're trouble, you know that?"

He brushes the back of his finger across my cheek. "You're beautiful."

"I'm probably a mess."

"I've always loved you more when you're a mess."

I clamp my mouth shut as a rush of excitement runs through me. King seems to know exactly what he just said, and there's no embarrassment or hesitation in his eyes. "That's a big word," I mutter. And it's one I haven't heard him say in almost a decade.

He nods. "I know."

I need to say something in return—he's clearly waiting and hoping for it—but all of my words catch in my throat. Yesterday, it was easy to think I could be happy here for the rest of my life, but in the light of a new day, all of my old fears come creeping back in.

I press my palm to his cheek. "Let's see what's going on at the bakery, and then we can talk. Okay?"

He nods again, but I don't miss the disappointment in his eyes before he sits up.

When we get to the bakery half an hour later, there's quite a crowd gathered around the doors. Whoever is inside, he's drawn a lot of attention, and I really hope it's something good and not some kind of impending disaster. The knot in my stomach seems to think I'm not going to like what's inside.

Holding King's hand a little tighter, I start working my way through the crowd. Some of them are locals, and they're quick to make room when they see us, but the tourists are more interested in the man inside than the two people trying to get past them.

I'm ready to start shouting by the time I reach the doors—I could still be in bed with my husband, but I'm stuck squeezing past sweaty Northerners because I wasn't smart enough to use the back door. Even if this mystery person is someone good, I'm not going to be happy about him disrupting my morning.

I finally stumble inside, King right behind me. Through the mass of people in the lobby, I see the cameraman first, and the knot doubles in size because I recognize him. I recognize the man next to him even more.

"You've got to be kidding," I breathe. "Lane?"

Lane jumps to his feet when he sees me over the heads of the crowd. "Georgie!"

Ned, one of the cameramen from *Home Baked*, quickly lifts his camera to his shoulder and starts filming.

"The idiot ex?" King asks quietly as Lane starts making his way across the lobby. "How do you want to handle this?"

I can't decide if he's asking what methods I want to use to throw my ex out of the bakery or if he's really wondering if I might still harbor some feelings for the jerk, so I do my best to be as clear as possible with the limited time I have before Lane reaches us.

"I'm probably going to need you to hold me back from punching him in the nose. But I'll see what he has to say before we kick him out."

"'We,'" King repeats with a grin.

"Follow my lead?"

"Always."

"Georgie, I'm so glad I finally found you!" Lane wraps his arms around me, ripping my hand out of King's as he turns us to give the camera a better angle. "I've been worried sick about you ever since I heard you left New York."

I've been in Willow Cove for almost two weeks now. It's been nearly a month since we last talked. "My phone number hasn't changed," I say, squirming out of his almost suffocating hold.

Lane puts his hands on my shoulders. "I'm lucky Cecily told me where you went."

"Didn't do that," Cecily says. For some reason, she's behind the counter with Emily, the pair of them scowling at Lane. Meg, on the other hand, seems to be enjoying this little show as she leans against the door frame of the swinging door. "I want it on the record that I specifically told you that you can stick your so-called apology up your—"

"You came to apologize?" If I sound shocked, it's because I am. I don't think Lane has ever apologized to me. Not in so many words, anyway. He has a knack for saying things that *sound* like an apology but ultimately put the blame anywhere but on himself.

Lane nods almost theatrically. "The way things went down, I couldn't... I didn't want to break up with you, Georgie."

I fold my arms and take a step back so his hands fall from my shoulders. "Okay. So when you said we were going in different directions and that you couldn't keep letting me hold you back, that was...not a breakup?"

"That was me being an idiot."

"I agree with you there."

"Georgie." He glances at the camera and then steps in close, dropping his voice to a low murmur. I would believe he really means for what he says to be private if not for the microphone pinned to his collar. "I didn't want to break up with you. It was the network. They thought we were too perfect of a couple and that maybe a little drama would spice things up again. It was never supposed to be permanent."

I lift an eyebrow. While I can't see King behind me, I can practically feel the anger rolling off him in waves. I really hope Ned is keeping King in the frame because this is going to make television gold if Lane keeps being the idiot that he is. "Okay," I say again, pretending to understand his logic. "And how was kicking me off the show supposed to get us back together?"

Lane's mask slips for a second, like he didn't expect me to question his reasoning. "Oh. Well, obviously it was going to be a victorious comeback. Make our viewers miss you before you return as the triumphant hero."

"I don't see what's triumphant about being dumped on live television."

Frustration sparks to life in his eyes. It's a familiar sight, and suddenly I'm wondering why I ever thought it was worth trying to make things work with him. He's never looked at me the way King does, like just having me nearby makes his life better. Lane has only ever cared about himself.

"I told you," he says. "It wasn't a real breakup."

"Maybe you should have told me that *before* you dumped me."

"But then it wouldn't have been authentic."

"Why are you here, Lane?"

He huffs a quick sigh, looking around the bakery as if seeing it for the first time. He was probably too busy enjoying the attention of his fans to really take in the space I've been spending all my time, but he's seeing it now. And he clearly doesn't like what he sees. "I'm here to get you out of this dump, obviously. *Home Baked* isn't the same without you."

I laugh, though I don't feel especially amused. "I know. That's because the only reason our show did well is because I was on it. Let me guess—you've been doing old recipes since I left? Rehashing the few things you actually know how to make?"

Color splotches in his face as a murmur spreads through the lobby and out the door. "I don't know what you're talking about."

I grin as an actual sense of triumph and vindication bursts to life inside me. "You're not even filming new episodes, are you?" I guess. "They're just doing reruns."

"Georgie." He's starting to sound a little desperate. "I need you back in New York, babe. No one can do what you do, believe me."

I gasp when I realize what he's really saying. "You tried to replace me, didn't you?"

He pales, glancing at the camera again. This time in fear. "I didn't—that's not what I..."

"Did you find her before or after you dumped me?"

"Georgie."

"And were you just replacing me as your *baking* partner, or..." I quickly realize I don't need an answer to that question, and I shake my head. If Lane cheated on me, it's all the better that I'm free of him. "Honestly, Lane, I'm glad you did what you did because I am way happier here than I ever was with you."

He scoffs. "In a piece of junk bakery in Nowhereville? This dump is falling apart and looks like it's one health inspection shy of getting shut down anyway."

"This *dump* is my most favorite place in the world," I snap back at him. "It always has been. And if you had ever pulled your head out of your butt once in a while, you would have known that about me. I talked about Kingston's all the time. Even on the show!"

"You did?" King's warm voice cuts through my tirade, knocking my anger down to a simmer rather than threatening to boil over.

I turn to face him, my smile hesitant. He is an exact opposite of Lane, both in appearance and personality, and I can't believe I ever thought anyone else could take his place in my life. "Of course I talked about Kingston's. I've never been shy about where I learned it all. I like being true to my roots."

"Georgie," Lane says sharply, and it's clear his patience is gone. "I know you're all 'hometown quaint' and 'average is beautiful' and all that, but you really need to leave behind the quirks at some point and grow up. You're not hot enough to sell the cutesy crap for much longer, and no one will take you seriously if you don't move on."

Wow.

I put a hand on King's chest at the same time he takes a step forward with fury. This man's mama raised him to respect women, a lesson Lane clearly didn't get in his life. But I don't need King to fight this battle for me. Though King is clenching his jaw too hard to speak, I can read his thoughts in his eyes clear enough. If I asked him to, he would pummel my ex-boyfriend in perfect view of the rolling camera, and he would do it with a smile.

"Hey," I whisper, still pressing my hand to his chest. "I'm fine. Lane is just covering his embarrassment with anger. He's not hurting me."

There are so many emotions in King's eyes as he studies my face, most of them warm and comforting as his focus turns fully to me. He's not a violent person, and it's obvious he would rather end this conversation and move on to the one we need to have with each other. "Lane is an idiot."

"Yeah, he is."

"Georgie," Lane says, trying to get my attention again. I look at him, but he's too busy glaring at King as if he's only just realizing there's a man standing behind me. "Hey, buddy, that's my girlfriend you're undressing with your eyes. Only I get to do that."

King doesn't flinch. He doesn't even look away from me. "That's my *wife* you're demeaning, and you don't *get* to do anything. I'm going to have to ask you to leave before you insult her any further."

Lane scoffs. "She's not your wife."

King and I hold up our ring fingers in unison, which makes me snort out a laugh. "I was so tempted to hold up the other finger," I say to King.

He grins. "I'm *still* tempted." And then he covers my mouth with his own in a kiss that feels like it's as much a demonstration of possession as it is a declaration of his feelings for me. Now is not the time for this, given the crowd and the camera and the...okay, I don't care. I want to kiss this man as much as he clearly wants to kiss me.

I'm about to wrap my arms around his neck when a hand grabs mine and tugs with enough force that my wrist pops painfully.

"Georgie," Lane says almost frantically, "what are you—"

King moves so fast that I almost miss it. He releases me and then grabs Lane by the collar, tugging him forward and spinning him around. He shoves Lane into the wall hard enough that his head leaves a small dent in the drywall. "I asked nicely," he says in a low growl. "And now you've manhandled a woman without her permission, so I have no qualms about forcefully removing you from our property."

And he does so, ignoring the gaping stares of our audience as he drags my pathetic ex out to the boardwalk, followed closely by Ned the cameraman.

Cecily is at my side in an instant. "Holy mama, that was attractive."

I fan my face, though it won't do much to quell the heat pulsing through me. "Tell me about it."

"You didn't answer your phone this morning."

"I..." There are no ways to explain without her reading too much into things. "I wasn't by my phone."

She gasps far more dramatically than the situation warrants. "Then where were you, Georgiana?" My blush must give her the answer because she literally cheers, pulling everyone's attention back to us instead of whatever King is doing outside. Thankfully, she's smart enough to drop her voice. "I knew my marriage counseling would do the trick!"

It's my turn to gasp. "Wait, you wanted us to get together? We didn't do anything, by the way. The pool house flooded last night, so he let me—"

"Why in the world wouldn't you do anything when you've got a gorgeous husband who would obviously enjoy all the benefits of this marriage?"

I roll my eyes, not bothering to remind her how this marriage started in the first place.

She sighs. "At least my sessions made you finally see the light and figure out what everyone else already knows: you and King are forever goals!"

"But forever means living here in Willow Cove," I warn her, and for once the idea doesn't frighten me at all. "I know you'd rather have me back in New York."

"Of course I would, but most of all I want you to be happy, Georgie. King makes you happy."

The front door jingles, bringing King back inside. He looks slightly ruffled, his T-shirt wrinkled and stretched, but he's uninjured, which is all I care about. Plus, he's heading straight for me, so I can't complain.

When he gets near enough to hear me, I ask, "What happened to Lane?"

"I'm fine, by the way."

"I can see that, which is why I asked about Lane."

Shaking his head, he steps in close and picks up the hand Lane tugged. He presses a long kiss to the soft skin of my inner wrist. "Did he hurt you?"

A little bit, but I'm worried what my husband might do if I say yes. "I'm fine."

He seems to know I'm lying—he's reading my mind, like always—but he lets the subject drop and instead kisses my forehead next. We're still being watched, and I spot several phones recording us, but I'm not about to ruin this tender moment.

"I'm sorry about what he said to you," he says gently. "None of it is true."

"I know." I really mean that, even if King seems to doubt it. "But seriously, what did you—"

"I talked to him." King smiles a little and then presses a kiss to my jaw. It's like he can't stop finding new places to touch with his lips, and he's going to get us into trouble if he's not careful. We don't need to give the internet a different kind of show. "That's it. And I want nothing more than to talk to *you* now. Before this thing goes on any longer."

There is nothing that could stop me from having a conversation with this man right now.

As he threads his fingers through mine, King lets his eyes wander to the brand-new dent in the wall. "Well," he says slowly, "it's looking like a new coat of paint is going to be the first order of business when you start the renovations. How do you feel about an off-white?"

I snort a laugh and wrap my arms around him, holding him tight. I think I'm going to like this conversation.

Chapter Eighteen

King

I'VE LOST COUNT OF the number of times I've walked along the beaches of Willow Cove, particularly with Georgie, but this is one she's never touched, which makes this feel significant. We made sure the girls were all set at the bakery, asking a surprisingly eager and repentant Meg to resume command over the rest of the baking for the morning, and then I brought Georgie here to the quiet beach across from my house. It's not large enough for families to set up camp for the day, so it tends to stay quiet.

Quiet is what we need right now.

We've barely said anything since the whole thing with Lane went down, and I have so many things I want to say to Georgie. And so many things I should say but don't want to. Like how Vanderman happened to be outside the bakery and heard me tell Lane that I will never sit by and allow anyone to speak poorly of my wife because I love her too much to subject her to the company of anyone who won't cherish her.

Vanderman admitted he was wrong to question our marriage. He said he was following Uncle Bill's instructions in their entirety, and then he handed me a letter. My name was on the front, as well as Georgie's. In Bill's handwriting.

I won't tell Georgie about the letter until I've told her everything else weighing my steps down as we walk through the sand. If I am going to open my heart to this woman again, I need to know it will be safe with her.

She's the first one to break the silence. "I still can't believe he came all the way down here to try to get me to save the show."

My hand tightens reflexively around hers. When I realized it was Lane, panic rose in my throat, but the fact that Georgie was so clearly frustrated by his presence quickly calmed my nerves and shifted my energy to anger. "I'm not questioning your judgment," I mutter, "but what in the world did you see in that guy?"

She laughs. "At this point, I can't even remember. I think it was our shared dream of starting a bakery, though his dream shifted into something different from mine. I was too stubborn to give up when I was so close to getting what I wanted."

I don't love the sound of that, but I refuse to jump to any conclusions. "What did you want? What *do* you want?"

She drops her head against my arm as we walk. "Something to call my own. I've started to realize it doesn't have to be a big something."

That's promising. Hope blossoms in my chest, though I still worry it's going to leave me brokenhearted. She hasn't said she loves me, nor has she told me she won't leave when Willow Cove becomes too small for her. Summer only just started, but what will happen when September hits and all of the excitement dies down?

"Georgie," I croak and pull her to a stop. "I have to know. Why did you run away?" I'm honestly not sure if she will even answer, but if I don't get anything else out of this conversation, this is the one thing I need.

Her smile is sad, filling me with trepidation, but she also reaches up and presses her palm to my cheek. "I was terrified, Royal."

"Why?"

She shrugs, and her words come one after the other in a rush, like she'd been wanting to say them for a long time. "Because I didn't know who I was. Because I thought my life was supposed to look a certain way. Because I was so sure you could do better than me."

I choke out a strangled laugh. "You can't mean that. Georgie, you are..." I don't even know how to put it into words. "You're a shooting star in a sky of people who are content to stay as they are. You're the reason I believed I could have more than the small life I'd been living. Georgie, I would have—" I stop myself, not sure if I should speak the words on the tip of my tongue.

I take a slow breath. It's not going to do me any good to keep secrets. "I booked a flight to New York, when Uncle Bill first told me where you'd gone."

Georgie's eyes well up with tears. "What?

I nod. "Even after the way you left, I couldn't imagine a world where you weren't in it, and when you didn't show up in Willow Cove the next summer, I begged Bill to tell me where you were. And I bought a one-way ticket."

"You came to New York?"

I shake my head, hating the answer to that question. "Before I could head to Charleston, Bill told me you were happy. I had been miserable for months, and you were *happy* away from me, so I took the coward's way out and bought the surf shack instead, telling myself that I was perfectly content to keep living the life I'd known. Even if it wasn't true."

A tear slips down her cheek, followed by another. I've never seen Georgie cry, and the sight is painful. I didn't mean to make her hurt.

"Royal," she whispers, shaking her head. "I wasn't happy. I told Bill that I was, but I missed you like crazy, and I kept thinking I'd made the wrong choice by leaving. Being with you...it didn't feel real. Things weren't supposed to be as easy as they were with you, so I convinced myself that it wasn't meant to be."

Brushing the tears from her cheek, I take a few even breaths and try to settle the old fears that have never fully retreated since the day she ran away from me. It's time to be brave and hope that I'm stronger than I was ten years ago. "Georgie, I never stopped loving you. And I don't think I ever will stop. But if you're going to leave, I would rather you tell me now. Don't let me hope."

Her response starts as a smile, small and tentative but so very beautiful. "I've been chasing a dream for so long. But being in Willow Cove again—no, being with *you* again—is the first time I haven't felt like I'm running after something. I think...I think my dream is here. Something to call mine, that I know will never let me down."

"Kingston's can be anything you want it to be. The bakery is—"

She touches her fingers to my mouth, stifling my almost desperate words. "The only Kingston I care about is this one." Then she rises up on her toes and kisses me. It's not a kiss filled with heat or restrained desire like what we've shared before, but it's every bit the embrace I've longed for over the years. More so. It's a kiss that speaks of promise and a future and my own hopes and dreams coming true.

It actually hurts when she pulls away only a few seconds after she claims my lips. "I feel like I need to clarify."

I groan. "I got the gist."

But she shakes her head and gets a determined look in her eyes. "I made the mistake of not communicating last time, and I'm not going to do that again. You deserve more."

"More kissing? Yes."

She laughs but *doesn't* kiss me. Instead, she puts her hands on either side of my face so I can't look away. "I still want the bakery in my name."

Some of the lightness in my chest dissipates. "Okay."

"And it's not because I don't want to be married to you. I do. If you're okay with that."

I take hold of her left hand and kiss the sea glass ring on her finger. "I am."

"Good. Because divorce sounds messy and I'm pretty fond of you, Kingston."

Fond of me. Divorce sounds messy. I'm really trying to see the positives in what she's saying, but it's getting harder every minute. "Okay," I say again.

"I'm going to make changes to the bakery," she continues. I can only nod now. "It has good bones, but I need to make it my own if I'm going to thrive within it. And we're going to have to do something about Prince Harry's pen because he terrifies me every time I go out into the yard."

None of this sounds anything like the vulnerable soul-baring I did a moment ago, and while I don't think honesty is transactional, I can't deny I was hoping for more "I love you" and less "that llama is trouble."

Georgie's smile grows, but it's not something I can match right now. "I'm going to miss the city, King. I know I am."

Which means she's going to leave. I take a step back, but she grips both my hands and stops the movement.

"So I think we should take a vacation now and then, when we're not in the middle of our busy summers."

I swallow as I process her words. "Summers. Plural. Do you mean..."

"I love you, Royal Kingston. And there's a whole world out there for us to see. Probably some great places for you to surf that aren't in South Carolina." Her smile is a wide grin now. "But even if you want to spend the rest of your days in Willow Cove, I want to share those days with you. You'll just have to be prepared for Cecily to whisk me away now and then because she may be this marriage's biggest supporter, but she's still my best friend and won't like that I'm choosing to make Willow Cove my permanent home."

I think I'm crying now, which is ridiculous, but I can't help it. "You love me," I repeat. "You want to stay."

"I want to be in your orbit for a change. You—"

I cut her off with a kiss, but I don't have the same restraint she did. I'm greedy. I wrap my arms around her back and tug her against me because that roller coaster of emotions broke down what little inhibitions I had, and I need her body next to mine.

But something crinkles between us, reminding me of the letter Vanderman handed me outside the bakery. Though I'm tempted to ignore it and continue with what I was doing, that feels a bit like dishonoring the dead, so I pull the envelope out of my pocket and hold it out to show Georgie.

Her eyes go wide as she looks at the names on the front. "That's Bill's handwriting!"

"Vanderman gave this to me after I showed Lane to the parking lot."

"What does it say?"

"No idea."

Since I'm just standing here, staring at the letter, Georgie takes it out of my hand and breaks the seal, pulling the folded piece of paper out of the envelope. She leans against me so we both can see, and then we read it together.

Royal, if you're reading this, it means I'm gone. I know that's what they always say in the movies, and I hate being a cliche, but there's really no other way to put it, is there? If this letter is in your hands, it means I'm not around to tell you this in person, and I can't say that I'm not surprised. It seems to be the Kingston way, going too early, and I can only hope you'll be the one to break the pattern because you deserve a long and happy life with Georgie.

Georgie, I know you're reading this too because that was the point. This letter was only supposed to be passed on if the two of you have finally made your peace and accepted that you are meant to go through life together. I'm not a fortune teller or psychic, but I have known you both for a long time. I know you were and always will be better together, which is why I made sure the bakery would stay within the family. I hoped it would be a push in the right direction, and it must have worked because here we are.

It's yours, Georgie, and I know you'll make something great of it. I started Kingston's because I wanted to share a bit of happiness with the world, and when I met you, I could see the same passion in your eyes. You reminded me a lot of me. Sometimes, that made me sad.

I made a lot of mistakes in my life, and one of them was thinking a bakery could be more important than a family of my own. I had you, Royal, and while the circumstances were heartbreaking, I'm so glad I got to watch you grow into the man you are now. Raising you, or at least pretending to, softened my regrets. But if I could go back and do it all over again, I would take every chance I got to find a partner. Someone to share in the trials and triumphs that come with every life.

Georgie, when you left Willow Cove, you were ready to take on the world, and I couldn't have been prouder. But I was also worried. I worried you would forget what truly made your summers so happy. It wasn't about the pastries or perfect recipes. It was about living your life to the fullest and doing the things you enjoyed. Every time we talked after you left, you seemed to forget more and more how much you used to light up when you saw Royal. Our conversations in the kitchen were always about the things you did the night before. The trouble you inevitably got into. The laughter you enjoyed.

I wish I had tried harder to help you remember what really mattered, but we both know how stubborn you are. You had to learn for yourself.

You both had to learn on your own, no matter how much it hurt to stand back.

Royal, you were so afraid of dreaming bigger. I don't know if it was because you figured it wouldn't matter in the end because you're a Kingston or if you were simply heartbroken. I'm glad you finally found your way, and I hope you know by now there is more to this life than what Willow Cove can offer.

I hope you both stay, but if you don't, I hope you make a home somewhere that feels right.

As long as you stay together, I know the two of you can live the life of your dreams. I wish I could be there to see those dreams come true, but apparently my time on this earth is done. Take it from a sort-of-old man: don't waste any more time.

I love you both.

Bill Kingston

I'm speechless. I can barely breathe. I didn't know what to expect, but it wasn't any of this, and I can do nothing but shake my head as I stare at the words written in my uncle's bold hand.

Georgie isn't so tongue-tied. "*Not* a fortune teller?" She lets out a single, disbelieving laugh. "Are you sure this isn't some weird prank? Coop trying to get back at me for blackmailing him?"

Wrapping my arms around her from behind, I close my eyes as I let all of this sink in. "Is that how you convinced him to fly off without me?"

She laughs. "Coop is pretty easy to persuade when you have the right dirt on him."

"What kind of dirt do you have on Cooper Heyes?"

"Unimportant."

She's right, and I let out a sigh of contentment as I hold her against me. I don't want to think about Coop right now. I want to think about her. "Bill really knew us better than we knew ourselves, didn't he?" I say.

"I'm sad to think he had so many regrets, but he did have his own family. It just didn't look like they usually do. I feel bad that we didn't make things easier on him; you and I were clearly difficult children."

I press my lips to her neck, enjoying the fact that I can do this without needing someone around to witness. In fact, I would rather not have a witness ever again. "I don't know what you're talking about. I was a *great* child." Never mind that the guys think I tend to lose all common sense when I'm around Georgie. Life is more fun with Georgie. It always has been. "You were the weird stray who thought working in a bakery was a fun way to spend your summer vacations."

Leaning into my kisses for a moment, Georgie twists in my arms and then places her hand on my cheek. "I did think that was fun. But I also think Bill was right, and I always liked you more than I liked the bakery. I still do."

I capture her mouth again, letting the warmth of her kiss seep into me and dispel the last of my fears. Uncle Bill was right, and we're so much better together. Georgie seems to agree, wrapping her arms around my neck and rising up on her toes to meet my height. I can't get her close enough, and I pick her up as I continue kissing her and start moving up the sand. This beach is fairly private, but not private enough.

My house is right across the street, and I've got a wife to love in every way I can.

Epilogue

Georgie

"Bakers, you have no idea how hard it's been to keep these renovations a secret, and I am so excited to finally unveil the new Kingston's Bakery!" I grin wide at the camera, trying not to let my panic show.

It's not so much the opinions of my viewers that worry me but those of the man whose happiness matters more to me than anything. If he doesn't like the new look to the bakery, it might devastate me. I would have preferred to do the reveal off camera, but after the way King took the country by storm when the "Lane versus King" episode aired, the network made me an offer that was too good to refuse.

They paid for all of the renovations in exchange for moving *Home Baked* to here in Willow Cove. As it turns out, most of the viewers were outraged when Lane went off book and dumped me, and there was even a petition at one point to bring me back and get rid of Lane. After the way he acted when he showed up to get me back, the network fired him quickly.

He'll be fine. He still has his bakery chain, though I did some digging and discovered his sales are way down since I left. I've tried to feel sorry for him, but I can't.

When the network first asked if I would come back to New York to save the show, I told them no even though King tried to change my mind. It was only when they offered to move the show to South Carolina so I could stay at home that I agreed, and it has been a wild six months.

The renovations have all happened over the last few weeks of November and December, and contractually I couldn't tell anyone about what was happening inside until this big reveal. Keeping it all a secret has quite possibly been the hardest thing I've ever done. My husband has a knack for convincing me to do anything he wants, and he nearly got me to spill the beans a time or two with his skills of persuasion.

I don't know where that man learned to kiss, but he's dangerous.

I move to the door, which is decked out in Christmas lights and holly, and send another smile to the camera. "Of course, I can't do this without my main man." I hold out my hand, which is King's cue to join me in the shot. We had to practice this part half a dozen times this morning because he kept ignoring the stage direction to kiss my cheek and kept going for a kiss that is definitely not appropriate for family television.

Thankfully, he does as he was told this time and presses his lips to my cheek. But the look in his eyes tells me just how much he would rather go with his version than keep things PG.

Knowing I'm blushing bright red, I give him a quick scolding scowl and then turn to the camera again. "As you know, King's uncle is the one who started Kingston's and taught me everything I know, so I wanted to make sure I honored his memory. Our family has suffered a lot of loss over the years, but the best part about good food is the memories that come with it." I turn to King. "Are you ready to see the new Kingston's?"

I'm not sure *I'm* ready, but King nods and threads his fingers through mine. "I trust you," he whispers.

"I love you," I whisper back.

After making sure the camera crew is ready to go, I push open the bakery door and flip on the lights.

Though the lobby is decorated for Christmas, I tried to keep it subtle so King—and my viewers—could still see the full scope of the new bakery. The walls, once a dark and almost gloomy green, are now a cheery off-white that makes the whole place feel brighter. The haphazard metal tables and booths have been replaced by tall round tables and a few long wood tables for bigger groups, and there's a bar-height counter running along the windows so customers can enjoy buttery pastries with a view of the ocean. String lights crisscross overhead, and the menu still has a handwritten chalkboard feel but is now digital so it's easy to change. Beck did an amazing job with these renovations, and the bakery feels even more like home than it did before.

I know the instant King sees the photos because his arms wrap around me from behind, his hold tighter than it needs to be.

The wall of photos, which before had been an unorganized assortment taped to the wall, is now a collection of framed pictures strung up along the whole upper edge of the walls. I printed some of them bigger, like the one of me when I was thirteen or fourteen and getting my first taste of working in the kitchen with Bill. I enlarged the one of King and Bill with their surfboards as well. My favorite picture is one I hadn't even realized existed until I found it tucked in the back of a drawer in the office, and that one has its own spot behind the front counter.

"I wanted to make sure everyone knows how special Kingston's is," I say, as much to King as to the camera. "This bakery is about family and always has been, and I hope everyone who comes here can feel that."

The photo is of the day the bakery first opened. Bill is standing in front of the door, a wide grin on his face. Next to him, his younger brother has an arm around his pretty wife, who holds a toddler no older than two. King. Below the photo is a brief history of Uncle Bill's journey to opening his bakery, from a small-town boy who started baking the family bread after his parents died, to the man who gave me the world when he agreed to let a scrawny thirteen-year-old spend her summers working instead of playing on the beach.

"No matter where you are or what your family looks like," I say to the camera, though it's harder to get the words out because I can feel King's emotions overflowing as his hold grows even tighter, "there's something special about the kitchen. It's a gathering place, and no one has ever been sad when sharing pastries with the people they love. Am I right?"

"I always love when you share your snickerdoodles," King pipes in, right on cue. He adds a kiss to my neck, which was not part of the script, but I'll allow it.

"That's because you're terrible at making them yourself," I say with a laugh. "And if you're ever in the kitchen, I'm always in danger of getting a faceful of cake batter and an impossible mess to clean up."

He shrugs, turning his gaze to the camera. I hope he winks and sends women everywhere swooning, but I can't see him. "What can I say? There are few things more attractive than Georgie in a kitchen. She's almost as irresistible as her baking."

I laugh. "Speaking of baking, I can't wait to show you my new kitchen. It is absolutely gorgeous!"

By the time filming is done and the bakery is locked up for the day, I want nothing more than to head home and crash. But the bakery reveal was not the only thing I planned for today, so instead of following King to his truck, I tug him farther down the boardwalk. "I have a surprise for you," I explain.

"I like surprises better when they're at home."

"You'll like this one." At least, I hope he will.

I keep dragging him with me until we reach the dock where Coop is leaning against his plane.

"I wondered if you were going to show up," Coop says, though his irritation is clearly feigned.

King furrows his brow. "I'm not sure any surprise that involves Coop is something I'll like."

"Ha! Good one. You almost sound serious. Now, I don't have all day, so all aboard or forever hold your peace."

We're quiet as the plane rumbles over the Atlantic, but the closer we get to the island, the more King starts to recognize where we are. He grabs my hand when the tiny island comes into view, but I think he's afraid to look at me. I'm not sure what horrible thing he thinks might happen this time around, but I'm determined to take the bad memories of this place and turn them into better ones.

Coop smoothly lands the plane in the water and gets us as close to the beach as he can right as the sun starts sinking on the western horizon. The winter clouds glow orange and pink, and I couldn't have planned a better night for this. I thought about saving this for Christmas, but I couldn't wait two more weeks.

Before we get too far up the beach, Coop shouts after us. "Just your friendly reminder that I've got things to do and places to be, so I will not wait around for hours while you two fool around in the jungle." He points at me in warning. "And you," he says to King. "I intend to leave with as many passengers as I brought with me, and I will not be blackmailed into leaving anyone behind in case you decide you need to even the score."

King looks at me, one eyebrow higher than the other. "Are you ever going to tell me what dirt you have on Coop?"

"Oh, it's so good! But if I tell you now, I can't use it against him later."

His smile turns mischievous. "I've got plenty of other info we could use. You should tell me."

I laugh. "Later. I only have so much time to get this right if we don't want to end up stranded."

I'm not about to take Coop's warning lightly. He's got himself a wife now who, according to him, irritates him to no end, but he seems happy. And I'm sure he's eager to get back to her.

If I had more time, I would take a little path through the trees that leads to a gorgeous waterfall, which is where things went down the last time we were here, but I'll content myself with the beach bathed in the golden glow of sunset.

Taking my spot in front of King, I drop to one knee.

Both his eyebrows shoot up. "Oh, you're actually—"

"Hush, Kingston. It's been ten years, three months, and fourteen days that I've owed you this, so let me get it all out, okay?"

He nods, a smile playing on his lips.

I take a steadying breath. "You were my first date. My first kiss. The first boy who made me think I knew what love felt like. When you're young, everything feels bigger than it is, and my feelings for you were so overwhelming that I barely knew what to do with them. And when you promised me forever, that felt..." I shrug. "It felt too big. And I was scared. So I ran away and didn't look back, and I have regretted it ever since."

His smile shifts into one of empathy. "Georgie, you don't have to—"

"I'm not done, Royal, so close that beautiful mouth of yours and let me finish." I huff a sigh of frustration, struggling to remember what I was planning to say next. Adding this speech on top of the episode was a bad idea, but it's too late to go back so I press forward. "I have regretted a lot of things in my life, especially settling for anything less than the unconditional love that you have always given me."

"Lane was an especially terrible decision," he agrees.

I glare at him.

"Sorry. Continue."

"Royal Kingston, being married to you these last six months has been better than I ever thought it could be, and I am so lucky to have you as my partner in life." I reach into my pocket.

King's eyes go wide. "If you're going to propose to me, Shortcake, I'm going to have to remind you that you're already my wife, so it's kind of too late to..." He drops off when he catches sight of the folded piece of paper in my hand.

I smile and hold it out to him. "I hope it's better than a proposal."

Taking the paper, he unfolds it slowly and then squints at it in the dwindling light. I can see the exact moment when he comprehends what he's reading, like a fire bursts to life behind his eyes. "It's the deed for the bakery."

"I got Vanderman to do some rearranging of ownership because it was no longer accurate."

His voice grows rougher. "You added me back on. And you're..." He looks up, swallowing. "You changed your name?"

"The world needs more Kingstons. You should never have to be alone. Speaking of more Kingstons..." I reach into my pocket again, this time with trembling fingers.

King doesn't wait until he sees the ultrasound. He pulls me to my feet and wraps me up in the tightest hug, holding me like he's suddenly afraid to let go. "Georgie." My name is barely a whisper, but that whisper says so much.

"For better or for worse, you're stuck with me now," I tell him and hold him just as tightly.

He laughs, the sound warm and comforting. "Better. Life with you is always better."

The End

Other Books in the Coastal Kisses Series

Crush Landed by Michelle Angus

To Have and to Scold by Deb Goodman

The Deal Maker by Britney M. Mills

Ship Fate by Dulcie Dameron

Also by Dana LeCheminant

Starstruck Love Stories

Moonstruck

Lovestruck

Love in Sun City

Kiss Me if You Can (a novella)

She Likes It, Hey Micah

The Chad Next Door

Crossing the Brooklyn Briggs

Houston, We Have a Problem

Standalone Romances

For Butter or For Worse

The Wonder Boys

Love on Camera

Love in Writing

Love on Display

Love in Disguise

Simple Love Stories (Sweet Love Stories)

Simplicity

Growing Young

Bittersweet Brews

In Front of Me

As Long as You Love Me

Dear Dalia

Let Go

Terms of Inheritance (Sweet Romance)

Forever You and Me

Holding On to Everything

A World without You

Love, Strictly Speaking

Historical Romances

The Thief and the Noble

A Twist of Christmas (part of The Holly and the Ivy anthology)

What Dreams May Come

This Above All

About the Author

Dana LeCheminant has been telling stories since she was old enough to know what stories were. After spending most of her childhood reading everything she could get her hands on, she eventually realized she could write her own books too, and since then she always has plots brewing and characters clamoring to be next to have their stories told. A lover of all things outdoors, she finds inspiration while hiking the remote Utah backcountry and cruising down rivers. Until her endless imagination runs dry, she will always have another story to tell.

Dana loves connecting with her readers! You can find her on social media (**@authordanalecheminant**) and on her website, **lecheminantbooks.com**.

Made in United States
Troutdale, OR
06/01/2024

20247857R00116